Another Slice of Life

Life Stories

Thom Gossom, Jr.

AQUARIUS PRESS

Detroit, Michigan

Another Slice of Life

Editor: Randall Horton
Cover art: David Paladino
Author photo: Anna Ritch Photography

ISBN 978-0-9971996-5-9

AQUARIUS PRESS, in association with Willow Books
PO Box 23096
Detroit, MI 48223

Printed in the United States of America

For my Mom and Dad

Contents

Introduction

You eat the pie one slice at a time.

The stories of ***Another Slice of Life*** reflect the decadence and newly found freedoms of the 1980s through the early 21st century. The newly hired groundbreaking African American Coach of the Alabama Tech Spiders waits anxiously for his first game. Jimmy takes his last ride into Hollywood.

Are they true stories? No. They're life stories.

The stories in this book are fiction. In the telling, some names of public figures are used. However, any facts, incidents and characters that may resemble real life are purely coincidental.

My job was to use my imagination to make the most of the raw material found in life, and that is what I have done.

Thom Gossom, Jr.

"Faith is taking the first step even when you don't see the whole staircase."
—Dr. Martin Luther King, Jr.

MVP

The whirring noise of the 16mm film spooled through the sprockets of the 1960s film projector, *clickety-click, clickety-click,* and *clickety-click,* the only sound in the darkened room. The film projector beamed a circular light, reflecting fast moving images on the old three-legged white screen. Two warring football teams scrimmaged in black and white, one team wearing dark colored jerseys, the other white. There was no sound. The film, from a bygone era, had the nostalgic charm of yesteryear.

On the screen, number twenty-two, glided across the goal line, nonchalantly dropping the football in the end zone. The referee's arms shot into the air, signaling touchdown! Number twenty-two's teammates mobbed him in an end zone celebration. A shot of the scoreboard told the game-winning story, Birmingham 22, LSU 21. The dark shirted team ran to its coach and star player and hoisted them onto their shoulders. The teammates carried the coach and number twenty-two across the field.

The beam of light in the darkened, windowless room revealed some of its trappings. The room was decorated in red and blue colors, the team colors of the University of Birmingham. The phone was red and blue, the television red and blue, and the walls, red and blue. Long dead stuffed animals, a lion, a wolf, a bear, a buck and a twelve-foot tall giraffe stood in arranged poses, staring straight ahead. A cabinet crammed full of shotguns, rifles, pistols, an Uzi and boxes and boxes of ammunition stood tall in the corner of the room.

A silent fan rotated back and forth on its axis.

Wood was the material of choice. A big wooden desk sat in the left corner of the room, a huge oak chair sitting proudly behind it, a throne fit for a king. Oak bookshelves and cabinets, filled with trophies, sports books, and hundreds of photos, lined the walls. Number twenty-two was in every picture. Hundreds of brass trophies, with little football men in running poses, occupied the shelves.

One huge ostentatious trophy dwarfed the others. A tightly muscled, bronze man, his leg extended at a right angle, a football lodged in the crook of his arm, stood atop the big trophy. The inscription read, "Collis Cannon 'The Cannonball' #22, MVP of the Southern Southland Conference (SSC)." Alongside the MVP trophy was a photo of 1960s Alabama Governor George Wallace and the "Cannonball." Wallace, in a quarterback pose, handed the ball off to the "Cannonball" with his blond hair, brilliant straight white teeth, and his Adonis body. A framed *Birmingham Herald* newspaper article from 1968 pictured The Governor and the All American Boy, "The Cannonball".

On the screen, the games continued in silence. The film footage was not the actual broadcast; instead it was a coach's reel with no sound, featuring play after play and highlight after highlight of "The Cannonball." He scored on long runs, short runs, runs around people, runs through people, and pass receptions. At 6'2" and 220 pounds, the MVP was a man among boys.

Collis Cannon was now sixty-nine years old and incapable of running to the bathroom. He often pissed his pants and wore a diaper because of the prostate surgery he'd had. When he had to go, he went whether he wanted to or not. His hair white, movement in only half of his face, body wrecked by two heart attacks and a stroke—he was a lifeless shell of the vigorous young man on the screen and he sure as hell didn't like it.

The MVP stirred in his oversized red and blue team colored leather chair. He grunted trying to right the dead right side of his body with his good left hand and arm. He pulled and grunted harder and a fart slipped from between his pale shrunken ass cheeks. The *brummmppp* sound vibrated against the leather chair. He pulled harder on his crippled, crumbled right arm, but his right side would not move. He slumped where he was.

Fuck it, the familiar thought ran through his brain.

He hated his life now. He hated being an "invalid." He often quoted baseball legend Mickey Mantle, "If I'd known I was going to live this long, I'd have taken better care of myself." The saying had been funny when he was a younger man. Not now.

His wife of twenty years, Janet, and kids, Cal and Cameron, tried everything to get him excited about his life again. There were his beloved football camps for the city's underprivileged kids. The Cannonball always made sure the poor kids got a chance to play with the pros and college stars he brought in for the camps. They loved him and he loved them. But now he couldn't participate anymore. His family arranged trips to the beach, football games in private boxes, weekends at the hunting lodge with his friends, but nothing worked, not even the pills. He was depressed and going to stay that way. Dammit!

"You think it's fun going to all the places where I used to be the king, in a wheelchair?" He had reminded them again this very morning. It had been a nasty argument over the drool slowly dripping down the left side of his mouth. It had infuriated him that he had to rely on one of his family to clean him up. He took it out on Janet and the boys, "I used to be the MVP. Do you know what that's like?" he sneered. "Huh?" he demanded.

His voice had grown louder. "You don't know do you? Well let me tell you. I was king of the world. When you are the MVP, everybody loves you. You hear me? Everybody! MVP, that's what they called me, M-V-P.

"I'm not the MVP anymore. I'm nobody. So no, I don't want to go. I don't want to do anything but be left alone to die.

"Go shopping. Get out of the house. Leave me alone. Go on," he shouted as loud as he could. "Do you understand? I'm tired."

Today was game day and as usual since his downfall when Birmingham played a big game, the MVP retired to his study and watched it alone. The family knew not to disturb him. The games made him angry. It pissed him off that he could not be at the game in the box with the other dignitaries, with everybody coming by to acknowledge him as the one-time, and still, MVP.

In his study, he mostly slept through the games. His dreams were always of his better days when he gallivanted up and down the field in front of the governor, cheerleaders, majorettes, and boosters with one hundred dollar bills.

Janet was the only one who dared to come into his private sanctuary and she entered only to periodically check on him under the threat of emergency.

Janet had been his secretary. He vowed to have her the day he hired her. She was a buxom red head with a nice round rump and stand up breasts. He had tried everything to get Janet in the sack. He arranged out of town trips where she would have to travel with him. He had her book their separate rooms next to each other in hotels. He took her on fishing trips, with no intention of fishing. But Janet played it smart. She would flirt, but she refused to go to bed with the MVP as long as he was married. For a man used to getting what and whom he wanted, it drove the MVP crazy.

On the day the MVP was promoted to President of the bank, he told his first wife, his college sweetheart, the homecoming queen, she was not his sweetheart any more. He moved his belongings out of the house and gave both the house and the beach condo to her. He kept the hunting lodge. He split the money and investments equally between them, with the exception of the secret stash of cash he had been squirreling away since he met Janet. His sons, Jack and Bob, begged him not to leave them and their mom. Now adults, they hated him, but nothing else mattered in his heart but getting to see Janet naked and finally making love to her. He married her as soon as he could. It was worth the anguish, heartache, and money.

On the screen, the MVP ran to his right, circled back and reversed his field. He faked a guy to his knees, bullied through another, and took off on a sixty-one yard jaunt, ending in a touchdown. He'd once again won the game and his teammates again carried him off the field.

For twenty-five years, after his last game, he was the MVP, on top of the world. But in the 21st century, the MVP finally fumbled.

In 2001, he had been indicted, accused of laundering money and racketeering under the RICO Act. The indictment, and subsequent trial, nearly killed him. He lost forty pounds. His hair turned white. He suffered his heart attack. The prosecutor, U.S. Attorney Jim Davidson, was relentless in his pursuit of "Defendant Cannon," as he always referred to him.

Cocky from the start, the MVP relied on his old football instincts. He fought from his gut and quickly wasted a fortune fighting every subpoena, deposition, and motion. He found out the government had more money and time than he did.

Newspaper coverage of The Cannonball moved from the front page of the sports pages to the front page of the paper, above the fold, the paper's number one story.

The news media, sports reporters, and all his old talk show reporter friends initially lined up with the MVP but they soon turned, with many of the reporters relishing the opportunity to stab the MVP in the back for the many times he'd been an asshole to them.

During the trial, with legal mumbo jumbo flying around the courtroom, the MVP would often drift off into yesteryear, designing football plays with the legal pad he'd been given to take notes. Every face in the courtroom was familiar, reminding him of some game, a touchdown, an old girlfriend, and the one critical one-time friend.

"All you have to do is... No one will know."

The words would stay with him for the rest of his life.

It was a mistake. He knew it when he had agreed. It was only supposed to happen one time. Why had he let Reese into his office? Why? He should have refused to see him. He should have kicked him out.

Reese Willis was an old college teammate, a half-ass player who was eventually kicked off the team for dealing marijuana and being a drunk. The MVP owed him.

Reese had plenty of pocket money in college, from his dealing and stealing. When the MVP knocked up a Phi Mu, Reese gave him the money to get her "fixed." The MVP told Reese, "You saved me from a life of misery." Reese never let him forget it.

Reese owned a construction company that didn't make money. The first time Reese asked for a loan he didn't qualify for, the MVP reasoned that one loan wouldn't hurt. After all, he was the bank president.

But then there were other loans and...

In the trial of the young 21st century, THE UNITED STATES OF AMERICA VS COLLIS CANNON, the MVP did it again. He crossed the goal line just ahead of his pursuers when he was found NOT GUILTY!

The MVP beat the system with help from the judge's narrowly defined interpretations of the law and his last minute instructions to the jury. There was also another development. One the MVP denied any knowledge of. The prosecution's star witness, Reese Willis, was found dead before he could testify.

The story in the local newspaper was that Reese had ripped off a drug dealer and couldn't pay his debt. Reese was found in a downtown alleyway, his head lay open like a ripe cantaloupe. Police called it a drug related murder.

U.S. Attorney Davidson was furious. He couldn't prove his case. The Cannonball walked. Davidson vowed to get "the crippled son of a bitch if it's the last thing I do."

The *Birmingham Herald*'s front-page photo was the Cannon family embracing in the courtroom under the headline, *Touchdown!*

It was a hollow victory.

When he was indicted, he was given a leave of absence from the bank, the indictment being bad publicity. When he won, the bank did not ask him back. They cut his salary, made him a "stay at home, don't come around here, consultant." They gave him an office and a secretary downtown, in the black section of town. He had nothing to do.

He disappeared from the newspapers and talk shows. He was reduced to an occasional, *What happened to "The Cannonball"* story, or he was the answer to a trivia question in a blog by some twenty-year old who didn't have a clue. The MVP wasn't welcome in the President's box at games anymore. He was politely and discreetly asked, in the way these things are done in Birmingham, to resign from the Country Club, Rotary Club and even his symbolic chairmanship on the board at Habitat for Humanity.

Janet stuck by him. When the MVP slipped into his depression, Janet did not leave her husband's side. When he was ready to eat, she fed him. When he wanted her, she gave herself to him.

Cal and Cameron were in court everyday. The boys worked hard to earn their dad's affection. They played high school ball, to please him. Cal hated it. Cameron loved it because it made his dad love him more than Cal. Cameron was planning to walk on at Birmingham the next fall.

But The MVP retreated. He grew more insular. His health waned. He spent more time in his study. The study became off limits, with only Janet daring to go behind those closed walls.

He refused to leave home unless he absolutely had to. He could no longer face the public that no longer loved him. Hell, they treated him like he was guilty.

. . . . .

He'd agreed with Reese to launder the money.

He did not use that word. He told Reese he would "take care of it." He reasoned he was not doing anything illegal. He had no intention of doing anything illegal. He needed to help his old friend and he would figure out some way of doing it. But Davidson got to Reese and Reese, looking at 40 years in prison, flipped on the MVP.

Luckily the MVP still had most of the cash he had not been able to "clean" when he was indicted. When Reese flipped on him, he used $200,000 to level the playing field in the courtroom. Maybe he wasn't "The Cannonball" anymore but $200,000 spoke loudly in what was viewed by many in legal circles as a pissing match between an egotistical ex-football player and the equally egotistical prosecutor out to get him.

The Cannonball still had friends even if he had to buy them.

The rest of the money, another $700,000, would be left to Janet when the time came. He had hidden it in a secret compartment in a secret place. Janet would know.

. . . . .

The first heart attack slammed him into him like a strong side linebacker. The tightness in his chest pinned him on the bed, his feet kicking in the air. He survived, but there were pills, doctor visits, rehab, checkups, a motorized cart to drive around in, and more pills. He lost weight. Stress weighed on him.

The second heart attack sacked him and the stroke nearly took him out of the game. The MVP wished he were dead but the left side of his body, as strong as a horse, would not cooperate.

The latest news would surely kill him.

Gary Stanback, the MVP's longtime attorney and friend had been the messenger. Stanback, even now, stood strongly beside the MVP. He loved the man with all his flaws. He hated to be the bearer of bad news, but he was doing his job. "A new indictment is coming down," he told the MVP, "Income Tax Evasion."

Davidson, scheduled to leave office in six months, took his last shot at The Cannonball. He would make The Cannonball's life miserable for the next six months, and, if he got lucky, he just might get the bastard.

Stanback assured Cannon they would beat this one too.

The Cannonball demanded of his attorney, "No one is to know."

"What do you mean," the attorney questioned?

"We won't talk about it. Tell no one," The MVP shot back.

"Your family has to know," the attorney counseled. "You are going to need them."

"No. Until it comes down, just you and me," The Cannonball requested.

"I'm not going through that bullshit again. Can't do it."

His mind made up, the MVP sent Janet off on a daylong shopping spree. The boys were going to the game. No one would bother him for at least the next three hours.

If only he could be the MVP again. If he could he'd just disappear. If only…

He'd gotten the gun out earlier. It was loaded. He would call Stan back and tell him to keep Janet away from the house. He wished for another way. He didn't want Janet to have to clean up his mess.

On the screen, the MVP busted through an opponent's weak arm tackle. He ran over an eager linebacker and then outran every other defender to the end zone. Touchdown!

It was time!

He heard the noise, the bustling and rustling of Janet and her packages. She was back. She was early. Damn! He reached for the gun and simultaneously felt the familiar tightening in his chest. The flash of pain was more severe than before. His muscles tightened. His breath went short. Fear shot through him, setting off alarms and panic within him. Sweat started to pour down his face. He aimed the gun for his head. The gun fell from his trembling hand. Landing on the floor.

This was no false alarm.

He couldn't move.

He wanted Janet. He wanted Janet and the boys. He was scared.

He did not want to kill himself.

He saw the flash of white light. He saw his long dead mother and father. It was time. He knew it. He slowed down his racing brain. He calmed his fear. *I'm the MVP,* he thought.

The projector continued running, *clickity-click, clickity-click,* and *clickity-click.* The whirring fan silently rotated back and forth. On the screen the MVP recognized his image and smiled with the good side of his face. The game was nearly over. Time was ticking off the clock.

He laid his head back against the now cold leather of the chair. He took a deep breath, pulling in as much air as he could. He closed his eyes. On the screen, The Cannonball, The MVP, crossed the goal line for the final time. Touchdown!

Church

The choir, sixty strong, swayed back and forth, their maroon colored robes billowing majestically. Their voices rose to heaven. They slowly, soothingly, ended a Seventh Street favorite, "He's Able." Jewel Jones, the Seventh Street songbird, a plump turtledove in her purple robe, her hair fried, dyed and laid to the side, belted out a note of praise that God must have personally handed down from heaven.

"...He's Able," the choir abruptly concluded. The congregation leapt to its feet, full of applause and praise, "You go girl," "Sing it Sister Jewel," and "Amen."

It was 11:20 on a beautiful, crisp, fall, southern, October Sunday morning. The southern sun beamed rays of hope through beautifully stained glass windows. Sharply dressed congregants sat elbow to elbow in every pew. Latecomers paraded in wearing their "look-at-me, you ain't got nothing like this" Sunday best. Jesus was in the house.

The portly Rev. John Thomas Brown lumbered his way to the podium. In his black robe and clapping his hands above his head, he looked like a Discovery Channel penguin. He clasped hands with Sister Jewel and Brother Ed, the choir director, and joined the choir and congregation in a rolling, swaying sea of spirituality.

Seventh Street Baptist Church was rolling.

Sweat trickled from the Reverend's forehead. He raised his hand quieting the crowd. The resulting silence came in waves, spreading throughout the congregation. The Reverend spread his big black-robed body behind the podium. He made himself comfortable. He grinned out at the congregation. He unchained his grandfather's gold, one hundred year old Elgin pocket watch from his pants. He gave it a good couple of winding twists and laid it on the podium to keep track of time. His Bible at the ready, he faced out at three thousand of Birmingham's finest black doctors, teachers, administrators, business owners, politicians, post office workers, steel plant supervisors and their children and grandchildren.

"Amen," he cooed.

"Amen," echoed back at him.

"I love all of you this morning," he willfully acknowledged.

"We love you back," came back the response.

Seventh Street Baptist had more black college graduates than any business or corporation in Birmingham or for that matter, the state of Alabama. If you were a new black professional hire in town and you were looking for a church with connections and a mission of service, Seventh Street was the place. The new coach of the Alabama Tech Spiders and his family attended. H.B. McWilliams, the world-renowned photographer known for his historical civil rights photos, could always be seen sitting in the left front section of the church. The new educator from Chicago hired to run the state's leadership programs headed up the church's education ministry. The ex-mayor who'd lost his law license and spent six years in federal prison for misappropriating funds, sat among the crowd. There were forty different ministries. There was also a health clinic for the elderly and poor and breakfast for hungry low-income children.

The sanctuary grew quiet. The ushers stationed throughout the church, ensured the quiet would not be interrupted. The deacons and good sisters in their reserved pews and every other eye in the church was riveted on Rev. Brown.

The Rev. Brown grinned a boyish grin and began slowly. "We live," he paused, his eyes rapid fire locking onto as many members of the congregation as possible. Their eyes in turn were locked onto his.

"...in a time of technological advancement and spiritual and civil decline." He wiped his forehead with his clean white handkerchief, his red initials JTB visible to the congregation.

"Can I get an Amen?" he asked.

Three thousand congregants complied, "Amen."

"Let me tell you one thing," Rev. Brown warned, a trace of slow southern drawl creeping into his speech. He grinned as he always did when he needed to issue a warning. "I don't want to see, hear, or even smell..." he paused, letting the words sink in.

Like a good preacher, he repeated himself, "I don't want to see, hear, or even smell... a cell phone while I or any other reverend is in this pulpit sharing with you the word of God. Can I get an Amen?"

"Amen," Deacon Manuel Miller shouted.

The Reverend paused, eyeing his congregation. Members looked at each other. The deacons understood the Reverend was cleaning up some "church business." Ringing cells and teens texting during services had become a distraction. The deacons had taken the problem to the Reverend.

"Technology or no technology," the Reverend continued, "Sunday morning at Seventh Street Baptist Church is the two hours we come to talk to God."

His hand holding the white hanky shot into the air.

"Say what?" he asked.

"Amen," the congregation sang.

"Uh huh," he grunted.

"Amen," rained down again.

"Cause God doesn't need technology."

"Yes sir," answered Deacon W. G. German III, the oldest deacon at Seventh Street.

"Amen," cried the congregation.

"GOD does not need to go though a cell phone, a computer or whatever the latest gadget is to reach you," Rev. Brown rolled on, his voice rising to a fever pitch. "GOD does not need to e-mail, text, call, go on YouTube, Facebook, or anything else to talk to you. God, talks to you when HE gets ready."

"Amen," the deacons rose in unison.

"You don't have to sign up to be God's friend. You can go directly to God twenty-four/seven."

"Amen. Teach preacher," growled, Deacon German, waving his big wrinkled hand back and forth above his head.

"So, today I'm going to talk about distractions and I don't want to hear a cell phone or see anyone texting, during this service or any other service in this church."

Several of the older congregants stood up and applauded.

Lili Taylor, the seventeen-year old beautiful, Miss Teen Birmingham, froze, her cell in hand. The words hit her like a hard slap across her pretty mocha colored face. Her long smooth manicured fingers hovered above the keypad. The message she had begun typing was to Tyronne, her sweetheart, and a freshmen hotshot football player at Auburn University.

Lili's mother, Tracey Taylor, an attorney for the Urban League and widow, sitting proud and upright like a good Sunday Sister, gave her daughter an "I told you so" look. Lili tried to slip her cell into her Coach handbag. It slipped from her hands hitting the floor with a loud crackle sound. Rows of sharply dressed churchgoers turned. Embarrassed, Lili gathered up her phone, turned it off and shoved it into her bag.

Tracey disapprovingly shook her head at her daughter. The look was about more that a cell phone, a lot more, and Lili knew it.

Lili was having sex with a "hood rat."

A good student and homecoming queen at her private high school, Lili was going to Spelman College in Atlanta and then to Meharry Medical College in Nashville, at least that was her mother's plan. Lili would then fulfill her mother's dreams and return home one day a doctor.

But, Lili and the hood rat had other plans.

Tyronne was from the government projects. He was a respectable boy, hard not to like. He was nice, handsome, and had an interest in school. He and Lili had gone to the same exclusive private high school in Birmingham. Tracey had paid the tuition for Lili. Tyronne's tuition was paid by a scholarship created for "low income" students, who always wound up being black, talented, football players. As long as the team won, there were no objections.

Tyronne "made good," winning a football scholarship to Auburn University. Tracey had hoped that would cool the relationship between her daughter and Tyronne, figuring Tyronne would be soon stroking someone else's daughter on campus. But no, he and Lili held tight.

Tracey feared her daughter would get pregnant, but she dared not say it to Lili. "You don't want to follow this boy around the country while he is trying to play games for money," she had told her daughter. Tracey, a great athlete herself in her day, had done just that, following her husband and her own professional basketball pursuits around the globe. Her daughter had been born in Russia.

Tracey wanted Rev. Brown to intervene, but in his wisdom he'd declined, offering to let the situation run its course or risk driving Lili further into Tyronne's arms. A lawyer for indigent clients, Tracey, in a rare moment of lost patience, made the ultimate parental mistake of confronting Tyronne.

It was outside church, after a Sunday service.

As Lili's guest that Sunday at Seventh Street, Tyronne had worn a cheaply made white suit more suited for Saturday night at the club than Sunday morning at Seventh Street. He was an embarrassment.

Rev. Brown had preached that Sunday on loving thy neighbor and "what that really means." After the service, Tracey pulled Tyronne aside while Lili worked the bake sale with other teens. She didn't feel comfortable confronting the boy. But this was her daughter, her pride and joy. All she could manage to stammer was, "Lili has a future. She's going to medical school. You need to finish college and figure out your life." She figured that would delay any plans he and Lili would make for at least ten years. She told Tyronne it would be best if he moved on to some other girl.

Tyronne, hurt, and defensive shot back, "I have a future in the NFL. And after that, as a broadcaster," he assured her. His immature anger grew to a boil. He needed to score some points. "If I stop seeing her, she won't stop seeing me."

Tracey hit the fan when she caught the two of them having sex in Lili's room not once but three times. The sex continued in Lili's room, in the car, in hotels, and at Tyronne's uncle's apartment. They tried to hide it from Tracey, but like most young people they didn't grasp that their parents had been young once too.

"You're delicious Lili," Tyronne would coo in her ear after giving her oral pleasure. "Lililicious, that's what I'll call you."

Tracey made sure her daughter was on birth control.

.....

In the middle of Rev. Brown's sermon, Lili grabbed her mother's hand. They smiled at and held onto each other. Lili secretly prayed for the day when she would have the courage to tell her mother that she didn't want to be a doctor.

Rev. Brown preached on, "One day Jesus will say, come, you who are blessed by my Father; take your inheritance, the kingdom is prepared for you."

Rev. Brown pranced across the sanctuary. The church started to rock.

"Every man has to walk his own path," the Reverend preached. "And you know at Seventh Street when I say man, I mean men and women. There's no discrimination here."

"Amen," Deacon German, responded with way too much enthusiasm. Sweating, the deacon stood and waved his hand above his head. Traces of his natural white hair color, showed through his dyed jet-black hair, which had a purple tint. A vain man, Deacon German used an ultra jet-black hair dye on his head and his razor thin mustache. In the sun, it turned purple. Behind his back, the other Deacons called him "Zorro," after the television character.

Deacon German, a late sixties widower, owned German's Insurance and German's Funeral Services. He had more money than he could count. The businesses had been in his family for fifty years. His great grandfather W. B. German, Sr., had capitalized on a captive segregated market and made insuring and burying black folks in

Birmingham his way of life. It made him rich.

W. B. played the Reverend's words over and over in his head.

"Every man has to walk his own path."

W. B., a widower, had one son, Jonny, who lived in San Francisco. He and W.B. had not spoken since W.B.'s wife and Jonny's mother died two years ago.

The split had occurred over Jonny's buddy Larry Kirschbaum, a brilliant Jewish kid, from New York who had moved south "to shake things up" and things got "weird" as W.B. described the situation.

"What does the Jew want?" he would ask of his son. Jonny would laugh his dad off.

Looking to retire, W.B. planned the future of the company with both Jonny and Larry in mind. Jonny would be company president and W.B. figured he might as well utilize Larry's brilliance as the company attorney.

The bomb came out of left field. W. B. didn't see the forest for the trees.

Jonny and Larry were lovers.

"Oh my God," W.B. had exclaimed. He flew into a rage. Jonny took refuge with Larry.

"How can my son be a...?" he had asked his wife. "What did I do?" W. B. tried converting Jonny. He thought he could fix him. He brought girls around. He introduced Jonny to Tracey before she married and had Lili. But Jonny was hooked on Larry.

W.B. didn't give up.

He took Jonny to counsel with Rev. Brown. He asked Rev. Brown to explain the abomination quote in Leviticus 20:13 to his son. "Tell him the Bible says a man should not lay with another man," W.B. pleaded. "It's an abomination. Tell him Reverend," W.B. went on.

Rev. Brown, true to his contrary nature, sided with Jonny's right to live his life.

W. B. did not speak to Rev. Brown for two years.

Finally W.B. relented and admitted to himself that his son was "a fag," but he kept up appearances. W.B. would introduce Larry as Jonny's friend.

When his mom died, Jonny and Larry split for the West Coast. They were now "married." W. B. told people his son moved to California to get away after his mom died. But most people at the church knew the truth. They kept his secret for him.

Reverend Brown finished up his sermon. He quoted from St. Paul, "I once thought all these things were so very important, but now I consider them worthless because of what Christ has done."

He closed his Bible. The congregation stood. Sister Jewel walked down to the pulpit to join her husband, the Reverend. They joined hands. She began humming in that songbird voice. The congregation joined in.

Reverend Brown sang loudly. He looked deeply into his wife's eyes. He'd found a jewel when he met Jewel. He married her within six months of meeting her and swore off other women.

She was a perfect first lady, the perfect preacher's wife, with no dirt on her, unlike his first wife, whom he had married too young.

Jewel knew the Bible better than the Reverend. She convinced the Reverend to preach about secular subjects like worldly distractions and black economic independence. She convinced him to start the church credit union. She bore him three sons.

The Reverend and Jewel stood before the three thousand congregants, smiling and happy. Rev. Brown smiled eliciting a forced smile back from his favorite deacon and best friend, Deacon W. B. German. As always, W.B. sat alone, his money no recourse for his sadness. The Rev. sought out Tracey and her daughter Lili, who of course was back to texting Tyronne. The sight brought another smile to his face. He met the eyes of the wayward ex-mayor. The Reverend silently prayed for them all, just as he knew someone had prayed for him once so long ago.

He'd been a geeky teen that had wanted to prove how tough he could be. He was not athletic and he was not respected for his academic prowess. He had grown tired of his silly nickname, June Bug. So he did something stupid. He fell in with three neighborhood teens that already had a one-way ticket to prison and together they went to Kmart looking for the dumbest thing they could do. One of the boys stole some music and movies and was caught by the security guard who called a Birmingham police officer, who handcuffed the boys. Then the miracle happened. The cop looked into June Bug's eyes and saw something special. He saw someone who didn't belong with the crowd he'd been caught with. The cop removed the cuffs from June Bug and told him to run.

June Bug ran all the way to Jesus.

He changed his name to John Thomas Brown. June Bug and his past became a distant memory. In finding his own happiness, the Reverend was careful not to judge others. He loved his congregation, but he knew they like him were not perfect. There were times he let each of them solve their own problems.

He'd risked his friendship with W.B. by not chastising Jonny. He'd known Jonny since the day he was born. Jonny was a good son. It was W.B. who would have to make the adjustment.

Lili reminded him of her Mom. She would be okay, so would Tracey.

The ex-mayor had become more humble, a giving man. He'd done his penance.

The Reverend knew Tyronne to be a good kid. After a couple of life's bumps and bruises, Tyronne would do great things.

There were so many others who all looked to him for spiritual guidance.

The Reverend grabbed his wife's hand. He encouraged everyone in the church to join hands. They sang to heaven, "Silver and Gold."

Down South

The big circular balls of water rolled down from the older man's eyes falling over his beefy cheeks like a waterfall. Twenty years of pent up anguish made its escape from the deep recesses of his being where he had long ago tried to bury them. A long, low, wail rose from his insides, up from his throat and rushed from his mouth. "Awwwwwww, awwwwwww," he moaned like a wounded animal. The gruff man's big body retched and jerked from the pain. He held his stomach as if he might throw up. "Why do we have to go through this?" he cried. "Why God, why?"

The younger man didn't move. Sitting perfectly still in the junked up studio, he dipped his head, staring at the floor so as not to look at his mentor and friend. It was the first time they'd had this conversation and he didn't try to console him. He didn't talk. He decided the older man needed to let it all out. He'd never seen the older man cry before, but he gave him the respect and the privacy he deserved.

"Why is it so hard on us?" the older man continued crying. "Why?"

The two men, H.B. McWilliams, in his late fifties and Joshua T. Chaney, in his mid thirties met every evening in H.B.'s photography studio to work on the magazine, Down South that had been founded by H.B. as a publication for blacks interested in what was happening culturally in the Deep South. Both men held day jobs but the magazine was their passion. Down South was the mistress that kept them out nights past midnight.

H.B.'s photo studio was legendary in southwest Birmingham, Alabama's black community of Titusville. Titusville, a thriving, bustling neighborhood in Birmingham's days of segregation, still maintained several of the black businesses from those days. The busy thoroughfare, Sixth Ave Southwest, was the street of cafes, barbershops, service stations, dentist's offices and H.B.'s Photo Studio.

Although H. B. was admired and respected by the working class people of Titusville, he was not well liked. A grouchy know-it-all, H.B. was independent beyond a fault. If you wanted H.B. to shoot your child's wedding you had better be prepared to get out of his way and let him do it his way. H.B. didn't collaborate.

His photographs were works of art. Sitting for a portrait with H.B. or having him shoot your event gave you credibility in Birmingham. You were somebody.

H.B.'s creations lifted spirits and touched souls. Wedding photos and graduation pictures paid his bills, but he excelled at the shots museums craved for their exhibits.

The shot of the poor, wrinkled, charcoal black man one generation from slavery in Wetumpka, Alabama landed on the cover of Ebony magazine. H.B.'s civil rights shot of Johnny Lee Simpkins, a black man beaten to death by a hardened Birmingham cracker, hung in the Museum of Modern Art in New York.

Bored with the business of photography, but loving the artistry of it, H. B. started his magazine with two thousand dollars. He already had the dark room, many unpublished photos, enough business to keep his studio running, and the admiration of young, first generation college educated Black Buppies who wanted to work with a man of legend and get in on the ground floor of Down South. The magazine's market was black people with connections to the southern United States. That included southerners and others across the country. Most Northeastern, Midwestern, and Western Blacks were only one generation removed from their southern roots of Alabama, Georgia, Mississippi, Louisiana and the Carolinas.

H. B. was the publisher, editor and chief photographer.

Ever since the 1950s, when he hit Birmingham as a country boy with a college degree from all-black Talladega College, H.B. had given up on ever collaborating, co-owning, working with or for "white people."

H.B. wore holes in the soles of his shoes, knocking on doors for jobs but no one would hire him. The professional jobs requiring a degree were off limits. Segregation took care of that. The bustling steel plants of U.S. Steel shooting red soot into the sky of western Birmingham, would not hire a black boy with a degree. He had to be "uppity."

H.B. settled for driving for the White Dairy Milk Company. Looking like a misplaced porter in his white, white, uniform, H. B. ran from his truck, milk in hand, to his customers' houses, all over the black communities of Titusville, Goldwire, College Hills, and Honeysuckle Hill. After ten years of being the milkman, H.B. opened the photography studio. On his last day, when he was sure he had enough money to leave, he parked his truck in the White Dairy parking lot, walked out the gate and never looked back.

"How you doing boy," was H.B.'s customary greeting for Josh, a slight smile creasing his beefy face. Josh didn't mind the "boy" greeting. He looked forward to seeing H.B. Every evening Josh rushed home from his corporate job, changed from his Yves Saint Laurent suits, slipped into his comfortable jeans, picked up a chicken dinner from Church's Chicken and bee lined it to H.B.'s studio.

Josh's college degree from the University of Alabama, coming twenty years later than H.B.'s, and ten years, after Birmingham's civil rights demonstrations of the 1960's landed Josh a "position" at the local utility company. Josh worked in public relations.

Like the other black management employees there, Josh, one of the best and brightest was hired as a result of a consent decree the utility had signed with the Federal Government mandating the company hire blacks into management. Thus Josh, like the other black employees hired there, held a management position with no budget or personnel to manage. He and the other black managers joked that they had positions, but no power.

Still, Josh's position was more than H.B. could have ever gotten. Both men knew it, resulting in an unspoken friction. Josh had benefited from the sweat of other blacks like H.B.

Josh sold subscriptions and advertising on commission, supplementing his more than average salary at the utility. He wrote three to four articles every issue, his pseudonym, Ted Marcus. H.B. promised to sell him stock, and one day would turn the magazine over to Josh to run as publisher and editor. "You got a deal," Josh agreed.

.....

At first, it was one of the young women, Angela. One evening in a rage, H.B. lit into her verbally abusing her, criticizing her work.

"Are you stupid," he screamed at her, spit flying from his mouth and all over her face.

She walked. Her boyfriend followed. H. B. refused to apologize. A month later, all six of the young associates were gone, except Josh.

Josh couldn't leave.

He knew of the upcoming anniversary. It would be twenty years. He would not leave H.B. to face it alone. H.B. needed him.

.....

The loud ring of the phone startled the two men. H.B. stopped heaving, dried his tears and gathered himself. He disappeared into the office to answer the phone.

The doorbell rang.

Josh, sitting in the middle of the junk pile that H.B. kept on a daily basis made his way to the front door through the mounds of junk, film canisters, old paperwork and empty boxes.

It was nearly 9 pm.

Angela and Anthony were at the door. They had come to drop off the last few subscriptions and money.

The three sat in the larger junky room while H.B. chatted on the phone in the other room. The small talk quickly ran out. Angela and Anthony, uncomfortable wanted out of the studio as soon as possible. H.B. seeing them in the other room was in no hurry to get off the phone. He chatted away. He was smiling.

. . . . .

"We'll leave this with you," Angela said to Josh, handing him the envelope with subscriptions and checks. Josh wanted them to stay. He wanted them to continue to work on the magazine. Angela was brilliant with layout and design. The magazine needed her. His look asked her to stay. Her look said, "No way."

Angela and Anthony walked out.

H.B. walked out of his office. He wore the familiar smile. Josh recognized it. H.B. had a girlfriend. She made him smile like that. His wife did not. H.B.'s conversations with his wife were often short and terse. His girlfriend made him happy.

Josh waited for H.B.'s lead. H.B. didn't mention Angela and Anthony.

Josh did not bring up the previous conversation. He started to. They had never talked about it.

Silence filled the space between them.

The doorbell rang, again.

Josh quickly took the opportunity to get out of the uncomfortable room.

This time Josh smiled.

Mary, Josh's girlfriend greeted him with a warm hug.

"Hey sweetie," she said, in her syrupy southern accent.

"Come in," Josh whispered.

"No," she answered. "I'm on my way to your place. I'll see you when you get there."

Mary was gorgeous and smart. White, she was from Walker County, Alabama, which at one time, had been home to the Klu Klux Klan. She and Josh had been lovers since she was in college. He was ten years older than she. Neither of their families approved of their relationship. After all, it was still illegal for whites and blacks to marry in Alabama.

Mary would say, "Let me finish law school and pass the bar, then we'll get married. We'll challenge the law."

Josh would play it off, still unsure of their next move. Mary's dad left Josh doubting, wary. Something was there that terrified her. Mary had once tried to talk about it but broke down in retching tears. Josh didn't push. He didn't know if he wanted to know. They agreed to both date others, as a way of having balance. "We'll see," was always Josh's response.

"Want to come in and say hi?" Josh tried again.

"Do I have to?" she whispered.

Mary was another sticking point for H.B. Another one of those social no-no's H.B. would not tolerate.

"Be careful boy," was his advice to Josh.

H.B. was back in his office on the phone again. This time it was his wife. He quickly brushed her off with, "Okay. Okay." He packed his things for the night. It was close to ten, earlier than normal for them to be leaving.

He walked into the room without acknowledging Mary and Josh.

“Maybe he wants to talk some more,” Josh thought.

"Hey baby," Josh said to Mary, "let me speak to H.B. before I leave, ok?"

Mary couldn’t leave fast enough. She kissed Josh in plain view of H.B.

Josh escorted her out.

The two men reset themselves in the big room where they had begun before the interruptions. H.B. didn't make any motion to leave. Josh settled back in and waited.

. . . . .

He would have been Josh's age. The bombing of one of Birmingham's biggest black churches in the 1960s was the biggest news stories of the twentieth century.

One bombing stirred the conscience of the nation.

Sunday morning, was quiet too quiet. The bomb shattered the church with ugliness and hate. H.B. got the phone call. He rushed to the church. He found the separate pieces of his son's body throughout the rubble. H.B. went into shock, trembling, and whimpering uncontrollably. He vainly tried to put the bloody pieces of his son's body back together. A news photographer snapped the photo. It went around the world and became the symbol of the Civil Rights movement.

No one was ever prosecuted for the murder.

For twenty years, H.B. had refused to talk to the news media. No public recording had ever been made of his feelings.

Every anniversary, the first, the second, the fifth, and the tenth, H.B. had refused to comment. The twentieth was coming. The media and the public would want to know, how he felt, what he thought. He would never tell them. He knew if he told them they would fear him, and justifiably so.

The Today Show wanted H.B. to appear on its twentieth anniversary special of the bombing. H.B. told them no.

The upcoming twentieth anniversary of the bombing called for marches by the Rev. Al Sharpton and the Rev. Jesse Jackson. There would be a memorial for little H.B. and the other two children killed.

Since that announcement, H.B. had been in a funk. Emotionless until the earlier moment with Josh, H.B. had begun talking out of the blue.

Now, Josh wondered if H.B. would say more. He knew he could not feel the older man's pain but he wanted and needed H.B. to trust him. He wanted to feel like he was H.B.'s son.

H.B. loved Josh. He knew Josh could never be his son. H.B. had been down that road. His boy had been shredded to pieces by a white coward. H.B. would never, ever trust whites.

H.B., his eyes dry, his throat clear, studied Josh. He wanted to be closer to the younger man. He really did.

He wanted to talk to Josh. He felt close to Josh in a distant way.

He tried again.

Nothing happened.

Josh waited.

They both waited.

H.B. rose, gathered his belongings and announced, "Let's call it a night."

Who You Fur?

"Who you fur?" The silence shattered, the question exploded from the back of the room.

The participants had individually introduced themselves, all twenty of them. They were the school superintendent, an award-winning elementary school teacher, two construction company owners, several administrators, three bankers, two lawyers, several directors of non-profits and three local politicians. They were fifteen males and five females, including two blacks. Some offered their names, their profession and some tidbit of how they had been selected for this, the 1993 version of Leadership Walker County. They were the county's acknowledged leaders, some rough around the edges, but all able to manage well in Walker County, a few miles and many ideas west of Birmingham, Alabama. For the next eight months, they would meet once a month.

She stood before them smooth around the edges, polished and preppy. Her glasses gave her away as a fourth generation educator. She was doing what she loved and did best. Teaching. Leading a class of individuals to mutual self-discovery. At the end of the eight months she would see profound differences in them as individuals and as a group.

After giving them her name, Margaret Mary Comer, (she intentionally didn't use the Doctor title she had earned in education), she invited them to ask her any questions they wanted. It was her unique way of introducing herself. It had always worked with other classes and had often proven to be a great icebreaker.

"Who you fur?" the question again erupted from the back of the room.

"Excuse me?" she answered politely.

The stringy dirty blonde-headed, Elliott Smith, stood in the back of the class waiting for an answer. "Smitty," was the owner of ABC Construction in the small city of Jasper, a stop on Highway 78 West between Birmingham and Memphis. He wore blue jeans, a white shirt, and a dingy tie with work boots amongst his conservatively dressed, dark suited classmates. A sideways grin creased his pocked marked face, right below his uneven mustache. His eyes showed intense interest in the awaited answer.

The other participant's heads rotated back and forth from Smitty to the facilitator anticipating her answer. They waited.

For Margaret Mary Comer this was today's first test.

"Who you fur?" he wanted to know.

"I don't think I understand," she answered.

"Who you fur? Alabama or Auburn?" he wanted to know. "The big game this weekend, The Iron Bowl, Alabama or Auburn. Who you fur? Alabama's the favorite. Say Alabama and you can be my friend and be on the winning side. Roll Tide, Roll. So, who you fur?"

She finally got it. He was referring to the big college football game everyone had been talking about and she knew little or nothing about. She stood erect, her hands folded across the front of her thighs, perfectly lady-like. She answered, "I'm from Chicago. So it would be the Bears."

"Da Bears," he answered in his thick syrupy Walker County accent. "You can't be for Da Bears. You got to be fur one or the other, Auburn or Alabama. That's the way it is in Alabama. We don't care nothing about pro football, that's fer Yankees. Bunch of lazy-ass boys making way too much money. You got to like either Auburn or Alabama. It's a way of life, here in Alabama."

"So who you fur?"

. . . . .

In their introductions all the participants had boldly declared their football allegiance to either the University of Alabama or the Auburn University football teams, with the exception of Mary Hope, the local director of Workforce Development who declared for Jacksonville State University, and Jimmy Anthony, a country lawyer, who had graduated from the historic Black college, Alabama A&M University. Margaret Mary had done leadership training in four states and had never before encountered this phenomenon. But to the participants it was as natural as, "Good Morning."

"Hi, I'm Elliott Smith, Smitty. Been living in Walker County all my life and even though I didn't get to go to college, I've been a Crimson Tide fan all my life."

The introductions sparked rival comebacks.

"He's just a redneck from Carbon Hill," Joe Simpson a three-piece suit-wearing banker, blurted out.

"Auburn is going to win and he knows it so don't pay him no never mind. You know what Auburn and Alabama fans have in common," he asked in general to everyone.

He waited until someone responded "No we don't," answered Mary Hope.

"Neither one of them went to Alabama," Joe Simpson laughed at the top of his lungs. Several others joined him in laughter.

Elliott Smith did not.

Margaret Comer was out of her element.

. . . . .

She was refined and cultured, but had always been able to relate when required, wherever, whenever. She prided herself on it. Before becoming a consultant in her own company, she had taught special education classes and then high school. But the leadership development, training and diversity classes were where she now hung her hat. She enjoyed it. She had always made the classes engaging and interesting, always earning a five star rating from her participants.

There had been one exception, the Department of Transportation for the State of Alabama.

The class of fifty white male blue-collar workers prided themselves on just how redneck they could be. They were determined that this "little colored girl," as the supervisor had called her, was not going to run any class that they had been forced to attend by the Federal Government. She lasted one day with them and was never invited back. The feeling was mutual.

She had come south after her divorce, when she was offered a fellowship to continue her education studies at Birmingham University. It was a new start. In the first year, she flew back to Chicago as often as she could but she'd gradually gotten used to the 'yes sir', 'no sir' world of southern gentility, even if she had not gotten used to the segregation of neighborhoods, schools, churches and social life, along strict racial and economic lines. She'd grown up in the Hyde Park neighborhood of Chicago. She was used to an eclectic group of friends and neighbors across blurred lines of ethnicity, economic well-being and education.

In Alabama, she had briefly dated a well-to-do white man, John Stone, the president of his family's fourth generation jewelry business, Stone Jewelers. They started as friends. Then grew closer.

The relationship initially was exciting for him but as they grew closer as a couple, and the society talk grew more vicious, his father pulled the plug on the relationship. He threatened to disinherit his son. John Stone had never had much spine. Money ruled his world. He stopped calling her and would not return her calls. It was over.

Welcome to the South!

She joined Seventh Street Baptist Church and became a familiar community face.

. . . . .

This was the first time she had faced the test of her college football allegiance.

Smitty stood waiting. The class waited. What would be her answer?

"I grew up watching the Bears. That's my team," she again offered. "But I'm not a big football fan or sports fan."

Her words came out with a finality that she often had used when she would address her fifth grade special education class, her first job out of college.

"Okay," Smitty conceded, the shitty grin still plastered across his face. It was obvious he liked being the class clown. He would not give up. It was tabled for now and she did not have to choose. The class relaxed.

She uneasily began with the lesson plan she had outlined for the day. She divided them into groups and put them to work on a group communication exercise designed to show how communication could be distorted from one individual to another.

The class busy, she highlighted the words, "Introductions and Communication Exercise" in her daily lesson plan. She made herself a "to do" note.

She wrote alongside the headings, "Who you fur?"

The Parking Lot

The single beam of light from the lone streetlight in the parking lot shone down on an older, nearly deserted strip mall. Half lit neon, Mary's Beauty Supply, G's Music, and Big B Pharmacy, identified struggling businesses.

The lone, dark figure sat patiently behind the wheel of the small car in the dimly lit lot. The figure, a woman, strategically turned her head away from the light of the approaching automobile. The car continued to the nearby drugstore.

Another car approached. A long Cadillac, with a single figure inside, pulled alongside the passenger side door of the smaller vehicle. In the dark, the two figures cautiously nodded. The male in the Cadillac slipped open his driver's side door and slid his body out of the Cadillac's door and into the smaller car in a single motion.

"Hi, Baby," the man breathed pushing the passenger seat backward until it braced against the restraints.

"Hi," the woman returned cheerfully. Her day had just brightened. "How are you?"

The man smiled, "Fine." They leaned towards each other and kissed quickly but hungrily. They touched. They rubbed. Steamy, they pushed back from each other. "Mmmmm," the woman moaned.

"I got the job. I'll be starting in two weeks," the man proudly exclaimed.

"Oh, Baby", the woman quietly screeched. She wanted to do more, much more but instead she tightly held onto his hand.

Silence reigned. The looks said more than words. Chemistry danced back and forth between them. Arousal tingled in both bodies.

The woman broke the happy silence. "Want to celebrate?"

The man looked away. He wanted to savor this night, this moment. He wanted it to never end. Now they had crossed the line. He turned. Their eyes locked. Happiness gave way to uncertainty. Hesitation.

She knew it before he spoke it.

He said, "I need to get home tonight."

Life drained from the woman's face. Disappointment read like a billboard. She knew better.

The man reached out and took one of her small hands into both of his larger ones.

She slid her hand back out of his and turned away.

A car bounced into the parking lot. The man and woman slumped into their seats, both looking straight ahead, their bodies rigid. A customer emerged from the vehicle, locked the door and disappeared into the pharmacy.

"It won't be that much longer now, you'll see," he reassured her.

The word shot out of the woman's mouth before she could muzzle herself. It had been a mistake, but a natural reaction. She did not want to challenge him, not tonight. She did not want to have the same old fight. She was so happy to see him, to be with him. But the word raced from her mouth, "When?"

A flash of frustration brought a quick, sharp retort, from the man, "Look, I haven't made you any promises."

She flinched. He'd hurt her. He knew it. She knew it. The silence crippled the communication. They faced forward neither looking at the other.

Yes, she knew what she was getting into. But, how did she let this happen? How? How could she be in love with someone who slept with someone else every night? How could two perfectly rational people behave so irrationally?

She loved him and he her with a love that defied rationale. She had never been attracted to or entertained the idea of seeing a married man. But, this man was hers or should have been. She had known him first. She had dated him first. He'd been her first lover. But, she'd let him slip away. Her career undecided, she would not commit herself. Now she wanted him. She was sure.

He'd made a serious mistake, and he knew it. They had dated on and off before his marriage. They loved each other and would talk of marriage, but somehow, in the youth of their inexperience, it slipped away. They loved others. He told her he was getting married. She shrugged and dared, "Go ahead." He had. Now they both regretted it.

Now, they stole moments whenever they could.

They did not talk. Words could not explain. Words could not bridge the gap of misplayed opportunity. Words could only become slings and arrows.

Silence and darkness was their ally.

He held open his large hand and she willingly slid her smaller one into his. They locked their fingers and squeezed. They kissed for a long time, a deep passionate kiss. They tightly held on to each other.

The overhead light blinked off, the darkness giving cover to their love. Just as quickly the light returned shining down on them. The man pulled back from her and slowly let her hand slide from his. He slipped out of the door and into his car.

The Lady in Red

"May I have this dance?" His hand extended toward her. It hung there, an invitation to join him on the dance floor.

She didn't look up. She didn't speak.

Their images painted a picture. He patiently standing overhead, his hand extended. She sitting her head down, not meeting his eyes.

A gentleman, he waited. His look saying, "Take as much time as you want."

This was the third time he'd asked. The second time, she'd whispered in response. "I'm not ready."

"After the Dance" by Marvin Gaye drifted in from the speaker. Marvin's melodious voice sexually stroked the room.

Dance with me, come on Dance with me baby,
Dance with me
Come on dance with me baby.
I want you.
You want me.
So why can't we get together after the dance.

In a fit of courage, she looked up, meeting his eyes. Coy, she smiled like a schoolgirl. Her big brown eyes, like chocolate marbles, danced with delight.

He grinned all over himself.

"Yes," she murmured. "I'd like to dance with you." She extended her hand. He took it in his, bowed, and led her onto the dance floor.

The red dress she wore clung to her, accenting her figure. Her beauty radiated. She looked marvelous. It had been a long time but each step brought her more confidence, made her surer of herself. Other men noticed. She noticed that they noticed.

He took her in his arms. Their bodies melted into each other's.

She did not look around to see who was watching.

The DJ mixed in Chris De Burgh's "Lady in Red" with Marvin Gaye's "After the Dance".

I've never seen you looking so lovely as you did tonight.
I've never seen you shine so bright.
I've never seen so many men ask you if you wanted to dance.
They're looking for a little romance, give'em half a chance
And I've never seen that dress you're wearing…
…And that feeling of complete and utter love as I do tonight.

It had been a long and rough season of life to get to this night.

Dance with Me,
Come on Dance with me baby.
I want you.
And you want me.

He held onto her with no intention of ever letting go. She snuggled further into his body. She felt safe, like the first time and for the first time in a long time. He was virile but kind and gentle, like always.

He'd fallen for her the first time he'd seen her. She was beautiful, pretty, smart, and classy but the description he used more than any was that she was dignified. She had dignity. You couldn't get that at the mall or the beauty salon.

He leaned back and looked into her eyes. She blushed, revealing the twinkle she'd hidden there. He'd almost missed it. She had not meant for him to see it yet, not this early into the evening. But he had. She wrapped her arms tightly around him. He pulled her closer. He wanted her.

Never seen you looking so gorgeous as you did tonight...
And when you turned to me and smiled it took my breath away.
And I have never had such a feeling, such a feeling of complete and utter love…
It's just you and me, it is where I want to be.
Well, I hardly know this beauty by my side.
I'll never forget the way you look tonight.
I'll never forget the way you look tonight.

Others stopped dancing. They watched. There was something magical about the Lady in Red and the man who doted on her.

She laid her head across his chest. It was like the first time. The first time he'd held her. The first time he'd kissed her. The first time… She squeezed.

But that had all been before…

The nightmare season had been a living hell. The lump. The diagnosis. The surgery. The treatment. He was always there; every doctor's visit, every treatment, and all the counselors. And yet she was still alone. Had she doubted, yes. Hell, yes. She doubted him, the doctors, and God.

He never wanted her to doubt. He didn't. She became depressed, angry, and mean. She was ashamed that she was now less than a woman. He remained at her side. "A lapdog," she hissed at him in a fit of anger. He never missed a beat. He took care of her wants and needs even when she didn't know what she wanted or needed.

They climbed the mountain to recovery together, couples counseling, an occasional ice cream date, and many nights of listening. He made love to her as soon as she would let him. He loved all of her, not shying away from "the ugly," as she called it.

This was their first night out.

He'd chosen this dance in a neighboring city. It was for a charity they did not know or care about. They did not know the people nor the people them. He wanted her to be totally relaxed. He wanted his wife back.

He made her buy the dress. "Get the one that shows what you got," he'd encouraged.

"Or what I don't have," she responded.

He pulled her closer. They were one being in flesh and mind. He whispered in her ear. Her body responded. She tingled. She was a woman again.

"Happy?" he cooed in her ear.

"Very," she answered.

"Twenty years," he stated.

"Twenty years for you," she answered, "I'm not that old."

"Right, I forgot," he agreed. "I married you when you were twelve."

"And I'm only twenty-two now," she smiled a beautiful, "I'm in love" smile.

"Twenty more wonderful years?" he asked.

"Bring 'em on," she laughed.

They relaxed, now oblivious to the others.

He kissed her. She let herself go. She kissed him back. The bystanders, realizing they were in the middle of something magical, applauded the kissing couple they did not know.

"Can I take you home?" he asked.

"You might try something," she responded. "And if you don't, I'm going to be awfully disappointed."

He laughed his "I'm a stud," laugh. "You will not be disappointed, Lady," he assured her.

She was back finally.

The Lady in Red is dancing with me cheek to cheek.
There's nobody here, it's just you and me.
It's where I want to be.
Well, I hardly know this beauty by my side.
I'll never forget the way you look tonight.

Marvin Gaye and Chris De Burgh faded out. The crowd applauded long and hard for the handsome man and the beautiful Lady In Red.

He led her from the dance floor. She let him. Finally. They were magic, love in motion, dogs in heat, two people in love. They walked off the floor, her hand hooked into his arm.

"I love you," he moaned.

Her whole being smiled, "I love you back," she whispered.

Bittersweet

The white Mercedes easily slid off the Red Mountain Expressway and into the entranceway of Birmingham, Alabama's upper class, Forest Trace Condominiums.

Inside, Joshua, grinning in dark Ray Bans, his teeth whiter than white, reached to turn the Al Green's Greatest Hits cassette down to a soulful whisper. With Al crooning "Let's Stay Together" at an acceptable volume, Josh held the wheel with one hand, and reached for Mary's smaller, well-manicured hand with his other. Hands united, fingers interlocked, in peaceful bliss, they enjoyed a beautiful July morning in the Heart of Dixie.

Josh whipped the 280E into the designated parking space 14E for Mary's condo. While the engine purred, he leaned over and kissed Mary softly on the lips. She closed her eyes and returned his kiss. Heaven should be so nice!

"I'll talk to you later?" she questioned.

"For sure," Josh's eyes gleamed.

Josh watched Mary walk, bouncing on the balls of her feet, up and down, up and down. He loved her walk. "I love your walk," he crowed. She laughed, then worried.

Inside her condo she doubted. What had he meant? Did she walk funny? Was he being critical? Fragile emotionally, the thoughts danced around in Mary's head.

Sometimes Josh reminded her of Daddy. The way Daddy took control of things. The way Josh said he wanted to take control of her life. Ten years older than Mary and secure emotionally, Josh was careful not to criticize her. He was protective, strong, and in command. He was also gentle, loving, and responsive to her, nothing like Daddy.

Twenty-three, pretty, and socially acceptable Mary, had done all the "right" things, said all the "right" words, gone to all the "right" parties, and traveled in all the "right" social circles. Her looks opened doors reserved for bigger bank accounts and bluer blood. But, behind her lipstick smile lurked a roller coaster of emotions with few highs and many, many lows.

A college student past her graduation date, Mary lived with her sister. Pursuing a political science degree with no earthly idea what she would do with it, she had two semesters left and would be twenty-four, then pushed out into the world. She would no longer be under Daddy's umbrella. Was that a bad thing or a good thing?

What would Mary do after college? Law school? How would she live in the manner she was accustomed to? Who would replace Daddy's money? She could marry rich if she chose to. That would be no problem. She met men everyday at her job as a cosmetics salesperson at a ritzy women's shop. Professional men would come in shopping for their wives or girlfriends and would lust across the counter at Mary's olive green eyes, stacked body, and syrupy southern accent. If Mary wanted to be a trophy, that profession was open to her today. Would she try and have her own career? She would love to change things through the law.

What about Josh?

She couldn't marry Josh. That would be the surest way to cut off Daddy's money.

Daddy made his money in the coal-mining town of Jasper, west of Birmingham. Daddy didn't talk about how he made his money and no one dared ask. Daddy dressed in a fine suit everyday. He carried thousands of dollars in cash. He had an office, but what he did daily Mary and her sister didn't ask and Daddy didn't tell. Shady characters lurked in the shadows of Daddy's world. Beyond that, no one knew.

Saturday night card games in the basement of their house brought out "the uncles," plenty of liquor, and lots of money. The only true uncle, Elliott Smith, was their Dad's half brother. Elliott owned a construction company and was what suit wearing white people with money referred to as, "white trash." The other uncles were not related. They were Daddy's closest friends. The girls had known them and their gambling since their mom left many years ago. It had been Uncle Leroy who had liked Rebecca, and Uncle Robert, who liked Mary. If Daddy was losing badly and needed money, Uncle Leroy and Uncle Robert, would come upstairs and visit with the girls. "Be nice to Uncle Leroy and Uncle Robert," Daddy would say.

Daddy's do's and don'ts ruled the girl's lives. He never raised a hand to them, but they were terrified of him. Late afternoons, one or the other was posted at the door at 4:20pm. Daddy arrived home at 4:30 every afternoon. Whoever spotted him first warned the other.

When he was in the mood Daddy would laugh and act like a Daddy. When he had been drinking he would instruct the girls to go to their room and "look pretty for Daddy." Wanting to please their dad, the girls would try and out-pretty each other, with their best dresses, too much makeup, and a drenching of perfume. Daddy liked perfume, especially White Satin.

Daddy would slump in his chair and admire his two beautiful daughters as they paraded in front of him like adult models, one always trying to win Daddy from the other. Sometimes they wore swimsuits for Daddy. As they got older, they modeled underwear for Daddy. Daddy would get an erection.

Mary, at nine, and three years younger than her sister Rebecca, had to fight her jealousy when it became obvious that Rebecca was Daddy's girlfriend. Mary wanted to be Daddy's girlfriend but Daddy told her she was not old enough yet. Whenever Daddy wanted to kiss

Rebecca, in a girlfriend way, he made Mary go to her room.

When Rebecca started high school and wanted to date boys her age, Mary became Daddy's girlfriend. Rebecca taught her younger sister how to put tissue in her training bra so her chest would be bigger like Daddy liked it.

Mary remained Daddy's girlfriend until she was a senior in high school and beyond. She dated a couple of boys and went to her proms, but dating a boy just didn't seem right. It wasn't like Daddy. It was confusing. She went to the school counselor but couldn't tell him Daddy's secret.

Sometimes on Sunday, Daddy would take the girls to the big church in Jasper where everybody who was anybody in town would attend. They would shake everyone's hands and the church members would compliment Daddy on how pretty his girls were. Daddy liked when the church members referred to Rebecca and Mary as "your pretty girls."

From church, they would go to see Mother at The Home.

The visits were timed and strained. No one talked about Mother's illness. No one talked much about anything. Mother would love her girls one minute and the next minute she would strike out at Daddy. "How could you?" she would ask out of the blue. "You bastard," she would shout at him. Daddy, would smile, and pet his now ex-wife like she was the house dog, a pet.

Daddy had power-of-attorney over Mother. He visited with his ex-wife's doctors, paid the bills and made sure she had a private room. He would get reports on her social skills, and doctor patient privilege notwithstanding he always wanted to know what she said about him.

Mother mostly smiled. Many times she was as normal and sane as any other half crazed person. She played with the girls and told them how beautiful they were. She loved brushing their hair. She kept a framed picture of her and the girls by her bed. They were beautiful, the three of them.

Mother had started "acting funny" after Mary was born. One minute she was caring and combing Mary's hair; telling her how pretty she was. The next minute, Mother was in a distant land, either refusing to talk or speaking gibberish in some tongue only she understood. She refused Daddy's sexual advances, calling him "a sick bastard." She moved out of their bedroom.

There were loud verbal clashes. Daddy said ugly things to Mother in front of the girls. He called her a "whore," a word the girls knew to be bad. Mother started seeing and hearing things no one else saw or heard. She left but couldn't live without the girls. She came back, but Daddy legally blocked her return home. He turned the girls against her. The Home became Mother's home.

With Mother gone, Rebecca and Mary became Daddy's girlfriends.

.....

Mary tried confiding to Josh. She couldn't tell him the whole truth. She would be too vulnerable. What would Josh think of her? Would he leave her? Josh was outside her social circle but he was her friend. She felt comfortable with him. Still, could she trust him? Should she trust him?

Patient, self actualized, Josh was a listener. He made Mary feel like she mattered. Her wishes, thoughts and needs mattered. He wasn't just interested in her for sex.

They had the conversation about marriage. How could it work? They were both unsure and doubtful.

Daddy wouldn't like it. Nor would her friends. Did Josh have enough money? Risk-taking required financial independence. Not only was it socially unacceptable, it was still illegal in Alabama. Josh could lose his job.

Josh, a corporate public relations manager for an AT&T affiliate met Rebecca when she worked for him as a free-lance writer. They met for drinks. Rebecca invited Mary. Mary and Josh fell hard, electricity crackling back and forth from her olive eyes to his brown ones.

They skipped the dating stage and went right to hanging together all day, every day. Mary tried helplessly to keep him at a distance. It didn't work.

She was able however, to keep him away from Daddy.

Rebecca married and moved to New Orleans. Before she left she warned Mary that Joshua had come on to her. "I told him I wasn't interested," she said. "He's like the rest of them," Rebecca warned. "He only wants sex."

Josh and Mary did have sex, grunting, grinding, wet, fluid-mixing sex. But there were also long nights of watching television with him holding her like a kitten. He was protective and she wanted protection. They would ride to the park, hands locked, singing along with Al Green. He'd entertain her with his jokes. She would laugh heartily. He loved making her laugh and she loved laughing.

Too often her life had been sullen, fearful and turned inside out. She could slip into moods that Josh did not understand. In bits and pieces she would mumble about Daddy and her uncles. She would talk in tongues about going to see her mother in "The Home". She was fearful of becoming her mom.

Then one day Daddy arrived.

It was the way Daddy had looked at him, the long silent stare. A little man with pent up explosiveness. Was Daddy jealous? Was it Josh's race? Whatever, Daddy was not happy.

They had been lounging in Mary's living room. Joshua had his shoes off. Mary lay across his chest. Josh's hand was inside Mary's blouse resting on her breast, playing with her nipple. They watched "The Cosby Show." They were as relaxed and peaceful as they had ever been.

When the door opened. Daddy walked right in. He had a key! He stood in the middle of the floor, hands on his hips, looking, staring.

Josh knew the look. This was about more than race. This was about jealousy! Mary's Dad was jealous of her and Josh. Josh got it, immediately! He was in love with another man's girlfriend.

Because Mary was white and he black, Josh had reasoned they would never marry or go much beyond where they were now, but he had fallen for the girl and couldn't help himself. He had always expected it to end when the thought of having children would become an issue. But Daddy walking through the front door had abruptly ended it on the spot.

Josh rose to put on his shoes.

"Mary, can I talk with you in the back?" Daddy said. Mary tucked her breast back into her bra and straightened her blouse. They went into the back. She did not bounce when she walked.

Josh tied his shoes, straightened his clothes. He waited for a few minutes then reasoned, what's the use? He slipped his keys into his pocket and headed for the door.

Mary emerged from the bedroom her hair mussed. Her Dad remained in the bedroom.

Mary looked more fragile than Joshua ever remembered. Tears leaked from the corners of her eyes. "I'm sorry," she apologized.

Josh's brown eyes told her olive ones, he understood. Josh walked out the door.

Poo-Poo

As a boy, he had been slim, fresh-faced and innocent, a skinny string bean of a fella with a big grin, literally, the new kid on the block. As an adult he had developed that strong, country boy, look of his dad; his face was harder, containing more worry lines and the deep, dark wrinkles that came from street life, robbery and hustling.

The photo was one of those anonymous "deer in the headlights" prison shots of just another nobody locked up among thousands, rotting away, like peaches in a basket. The photo, a mug shot, was complete with a State of Alabama Corrections Number, 6378941.

This "nobody" was different. I knew him. We had history.

It had been so many years ago.

Studying the photo, I looked for clues, a bridge between then and now. What happened?

Was this "habitual felon" the same baby boy I babysat as a teenager? Was it the same baby boy I named Poo-Poo after he informed me in baby talk "poo-poo" and then let the green smelly slime go in his diaper and ooze down his leg?

I looked. I studied. I knew the answer. Yes, it was Poo-Poo.

It was April 1, 1990, April Fools Day.

This was no joke! The headline under his and another felon's picture in the hometown newspaper read, *Two Charged in Robbery.*

Cool had called from Birmingham to inform me, "Your little buddy made the papers. Look it up."

I did.

Police have charged two men with robbery and burglary, after a chase. Ervin Slade III and … are each charged with two counts of first-degree burglary. They were being held in the county jail without bond.

Police said the two men robbed a home in the Harper area around 11 p.m. and left the scene in a truck. Police pursued the men. The men bailed out of the truck. A police officer broke his leg in a foot chase but managed to tackle one suspect after his injury. Both men were arrested.

Poo-Poo had been a late child.

His parents, both nearing forty, ran a nightclub, selling beer and whiskey and chasing drunks until the wee hours of the morning. His dad drove a meat truck during the day. His mom shopped, dressed provocatively, and "ran around." She had "friends," younger male friends. His seven-year old sister and ten year old brother learned to fend for themselves.

At age 13, I was hired to baby-sit Poo-Poo.

As a baby, he was sweet, compliant, and we enjoyed each other's company.

As a two year old, he was rambunctious, all over the place.

At five, he became my little companion. Everyone on our street called Poo-Poo my little brother.

When I turned eighteen, I left for college. Poo-Poo rebelled.

He lost what amounted to his one adult friend. I could no longer console him, be his dime store psychiatrist. Steer him away from the streets.

Alone, in his own home, he needed attention. He found it outside the home. School was a train wreck. He acted up, choosing fights and bad grades over studies and good citizenship.

He beat a boy badly in school, hospitalizing him. He was hit with a three-day suspension. With his parents at work and the neighborhood children at school, he stole the sky blue panties of the lady who lived next door to my parent's house as they blew in the wind on her outdoor clothesline. He broke in other houses and stole more panties. His panty victims all had one thing in common, they all had big asses. In the close-knit neighborhood, when caught, he always got a pass. "You know Poo-Poo, his parents live up the hill," the ladies of the neighborhood would say.

Poo-Poo crossed the line from panty mischief to criminal behavior, without blinking an eye. He broke into my parent's neighbor's house during another school suspension and made himself at home for the day. He fried an egg, had his lunch, watched television, took a nap in their bed and then left his calling card, a lump of green stinky poo poo on their hardwood floors.

He was twelve years old.

At eighteen, he began the criminal's cycle of in-and-out of prison. He was never violent, just stupid.

His specialty was breaking into people's homes, stealing personal belongings, which he could easily hock, and any money he could find. If a woman lived there, he always took a pair of panties. He was known in the neighborhood as The Panty Bandit. He liked the title.

We lost contact for twenty-five years.

I moved to the West Coast. Occasionally word came that he was either in or out of prison. But there was no communication between us.

Then the letters began.

The first was postmarked October 18th, 1994. His name was on the outside of the envelope. It was his legal name, Ervin Slade III. The return address also included his number, 6378941, his dorm, bed, and cell, and the warning:

"This correspondence is forwarded from an Alabama State Prison. The contents have not been evaluated, and the Alabama Department of Correction is not responsible for the substance or content of the enclosed communication."

Sadness crept over me. I found the letter crude, repetitive, and full of grammatical errors. Had I failed him? Should I have been more responsible for him? Could I have done more?

I didn't want to write him back. I didn't want to go backward. What was the point? He was in prison. I was in California.

Guilt ate away at me. It was Poo-Poo. I could not, not respond.

I sent him back a note, telling him I was glad to hear from him and wished him the best in his upcoming parole hearing.

Within a week I received another letter.

Dear Tommy,

I have your letter dated 11-8-94 and I had no ideal that I was writing to someone that knew me as you do.

You see I've written a great deal of people trying to get some help in my area but never did they give me an answer in any form so I gave it no second thought because people have a tendency to look over letters from people; who are in my situation.

I realize I made a silly mistake in my life and I understand that this is not the way of life that I want to live...

I will be coming up before the parole board in March of 1995 and I've given them what they have ask for as staying out of trouble and being cool...

Like I stated I am willing and open to learning anything that's going to help me, I realize that I must change my surroundings in order for me to do what I got to do and I know it's got to be done in the positive force in life that's being around people who are willing to show me better and new ways of life.

So whatever you are willing to help me with I sincerely would appreciate it and I look forward to this and working with you however.

Take care and I'll do likewise.

Sincerely,
Ervin Slade, III

When his dad died, I was told Poo-Poo was brought to his dad's gravesite by a burly red-faced State of Alabama prison guard. Poo-Poo was in chains, leg irons and a jump suit. He was 30.

The letters continued.

Sunday Dec 4th 1994

Dear Tommy,

Things with me are fairly well. I am just trying to get things in proper and correct perspective so I can meet this parole man here this month.

...I've given them just what they want so far as staying out of trouble. I've gotten all this free schooling they give and trying to keep my head on level cause that is what I'll need to deal with life out there in the world.

I'm doing a lot of reading. I just finished reading the book title: "Succeeding against the odds." This book is a plus towards granting me new ways of winning and staying in the positive force of life.

I told my mama, I heard from you. She was surprised.

Once again I do want to extend my appreciation to you for being willing to be wanting to aid me and show me what's needed as I look forward to hearing from you as well working with you in helping me.

Take care and happy holidays.

Sincerely
Ervin Slade III

I responded to him with encouragement about his upcoming parole hearing and about his desire to work in communications. His prison record and lack of written communication skills made working in any professional field unlikely, but if he was willing to try, then I was willing to help.

Sunday Jan 1, 1995

"Happy New Year"

Dear Tommy

I just came from seeing my lady friend on the visiting yard. And I was sitting here listening to the Sunday "Jazz" on WENN and felt I'd drop you this letter with sincere intentions.

... I am a firm believer in "God" who sees all and know what's best for us as a people and I give thanks to "God" for keeping me safe dealing with the mass confusion of the system itself.

Dealing with people is something I must say. I work inside the prison cutting hair and I have to mess with all sorts of funny ways of people so I can relate to what you are speaking of.

My being in this prison has caused me to realize that this is not a place I want to stay. Yes! I understand that I've did wrong in my life but since I've been here I made a great deal of assessments within myself.

I go before the parole board in March 95'

Here is a picture of me just out and moving around. At a formal ware dinner. I am not little anymore 6'2" 210.

Once I'd written him, I realized this would never end. My guilt gave way to the question, "what was I doing?" I had known this kid up until the time he was seven years old. Since that time I'd only seen him, maybe, five times. He'd spent half of his life in and out of jails and prisons.

The letters had started to repeat themselves. I decided not to respond to the latest one.

January 17th 1995

Dear Tommy,

I've been doing a great deal of seeking into the PR professional. I've written the media representative for the Sierra Club in San Francisco.

I got a friend that's in Dallas Texas. She want to be a support system upon my release but I want to go back to my own city first and clean up a few things something like give something back to my home front. Never forget where I come from.

Sincerely
Ervin Slade III

P.S. I like San Francisco 49ers to go all the way. Have a good day. Excuse the marking out I realize it's informal but I am rushing.

There was something there. It lurked beneath the lines on the page.

The repetition. The false witness to God. There was so much not said and too little depth to what was said. I admitted what I knew in my heart. Poo's train was stalled on the tracks, huffing, puffing, but not going anywhere.

Poo-Poo was a lifer. And, he was not my responsibility.

After the next letter, I cut off the communication. The stabbing had been too much for me. Someone had died. It was self-defense, Poo relayed in another of his letters. I wanted to believe him. He did stupid things but he had never hurt anyone that I knew of. Still it was disturbing. I knew it would never end.

Poo Poo did not get his parole.

It didn't discourage him.

Feb 2, 1995.

Sitting here in the mist of confusion in this prison system I consider I'd drop you this letter.

I was hoping by now you would have acknowledge my last letter to you. …

Brothers

Fat huddled up, pulling his surplus Army Field Jacket tightly around his neck to shut out the cold. Here he was in LA and damn if it wasn't cold as hell. The temperatures were in the fifties. It wasn't supposed to be that cold, not in Los Angeles.

Fat had been in LA for one year. For the past ten months he'd lived with a woman he'd met at a neighborhood laundromat with her two teenaged boys, who didn't like him. Last month he had hired on at the shipyard in Long Beach.

The brisk, night air rushed from his mouth and nostrils. He had worked ten hours and his lack of conditioning was telling on him. "Gotta get my fat ass in shape," he thought.

The isolated street with the single intermittent streetlamp up ahead flashed a warning. In the brief spot of light beaming from overhead, Fat saw someone walking toward him. It was another man.

Damn!

Instincts took over. What was not alarming to some sounded off bells of alarm for Fat. Los Angeles had proven to be scary. The Los Angeles he knew was not about Hollywood. It was about making it through the night to make it to work the next day. It was about "one day" thinking. "One day" things are going to be better.

Fat knew what was safe and what wasn't. A dude walking toward you in the black of night on this street was not safe. He could be a young punk trying to make his name for his gang initiation. Fat felt for the hunting knife he'd brought with him from Alabama. "Carve his ass up if I have to," Fat promised himself.

Fat had been fighting since he arrived in Los Angeles. Arriving in downtown LA on the Greyhound, on the hottest night of the summer, with no one there to pick him up, was his welcome. Fat paid a hustler a hundred dollars to drive him deep into South Central LA to his uncle's on his Mama's side of the family.

The uncle, Henry, an alcoholic and Fat did not jive.

Fat tried drinking with him but when Henry drank he got abusive. Henry liked to strike out when he was drunk. He tried taking his misery out on Fat. Fat didn't play that shit. He fought back. Two months into his move to LA, Fat was hauling ass down the alley of 123rd Street with Uncle Henry firing his 45 automatic wildly into the air over his head. Fat ran until he ran into the corner laundromat, where he met Brenda. She took him home. He didn't leave.

Fat had gotten paid today. It would feel good to walk in the house tonight with a pocket full of money. Brenda would be happy. Maybe the turds she had for sons would loosen up some also. He would take them all to the Sizzler steak buffet tonight. Damn it, he and the boys would eat as much steak as they wanted.

This end of Martin Luther King, Jr. Boulevard was pitch black dark, the darkest street in the community. The solitary figure walking toward Fat was slender and wrapped in a long overcoat. He walked in long, confident strides. Coming straight toward Fat.

With cars lined along both curbs, Fat felt hemmed in. He didn't want any trouble. Damn!

Fat's street survival skills kicked in. Why was the dude wearing an overcoat? Shit, it was cool but not that cold. Was he hiding something? Did he have a gun?

Fat was a bad ass and didn't back down, but he was wary of gangs, young boys who didn't give a shit about their lives and less than that about anyone else's.

Two months ago, a drive-by erupted on this street with bullets flying through windows and ripping away at houses. A fourteen-year-old girl, not quite fast enough a runner, was gunned down, three shots to the head and back, a neighborhood tragedy.

Fat held on tightly to his knife.

. . . . .

Jimmy, the solitary figure moving toward Fat, was way out of his comfort zone. He lived in the San Fernando Valley but, like Fat, he was here for someone else's benefit. He was here to see his sister who he had moved out of the valley for her protection. He'd bought the house for her as a safe haven for her and his money.

Jimmy seldom traveled alone but in order to keep the safe haven safe, he withheld the knowledge of where his sister lived or where he hid his money. He generally drove around for hours before finally landing here. Making sure he was not followed.

Jimmy spotted Fat about the same time Fat spotted him. Jimmy instinctively slowed his gait. He shortened his stride and felt for his pistol. He was seldom without it. The business he was in demanded it.

"I hope this dude doesn't try any shit," he thought.

Jimmy had been a street hustler since he swiped his first car at fifteen. He'd grown up in the valley. His mother and father had moved to LA in the sixties, from Birmingham. They'd seen their neighborhood, Pacoima, change from a mixture of hard working middle class blacks and whites to being overrun with more and more low income renters, hustlers and many illegal Mexicans. Also in the 1980s drugs and guns appeared in the neighborhood like magic, creating an underground business that swallowed up the young men and spit them out either in prisons or in graves.

Jimmy had done a couple of short bids, one in Chino for insurance fraud, the other for car theft. He was on police watch lists and had just two months ago, been held over in the county jail. The detective tried for the major rap of drug dealing, but Jimmy was slick, spread his money around where it was needed in legal circles and covered his tracks well.

Still, Jimmy thought, "I don't want any trouble." He again felt for his chrome-plated pistol.

Gil Scott Heron's song, Gun, popped into his head.

Brother Man nowadays living in the ghetto
Where the danger's sho nuff real
Well when he's out late at night
And if he's got his head on right
Well, I lay you 9 to 5 he's walking with steel.

Jimmy shifted to full alert. He wasn't holding any drugs. He seldom did. But he did have $25,000 in his satchel to give to his sister, $5,000 for his sister and $20,000 for her to hide for him. When Jimmy hid his money, he only trusted his sister.

From years of experience, his eyes, operated like night vision radar, detecting every little movement on the street. His jaw turned rock hard. His chest rose. This could be life and death.

The sidewalk seemed to narrow.

The men were close enough to get good looks at each other in the dark. Each knew the other was there. Crossing the street now, to avoid the other, would send a signal of cowardice. Cowardice could invite a mugging, an ass- whipping or a robbery.

Jimmy, short and slender, extended himself. He walked on the balls of his feet to make himself look taller. Jimmy wasn't a fighter. He had guys who did that for him. He had guys who worked for him.

They would kill for him. They had killed for him. But they were also afraid of Jimmy. Jimmy was the man.

. . . . .

Fat could feel the cold, killing steel of his Jim Bowie knife resting in its sheaf against his ample stomach. He had thought of buying a gun, with the thought being if he ran into his crazy ass uncle again he would be prepared. But he hadn't yet. "Shit!" He thought, "I'll have to gut his ass."

They were closer now, only two houses apart. Fat let his hands hang down to his side exposing his hands to the other man in hopes of diffusing any possible situation.

The other man's hands were empty, a peace sign.

Jimmy removed his hands from his pockets, making sure Fat could see them, a return sign of peace.

Nervous cold breath exhaled from each man. In the quiet, their shoe heels clapped against the sidewalk.

They were one house apart.

They were within five feet of each other.

Neither man's eyes left the other. Like hawks, they eyed the other's slightest move. Neither man did anything to threaten the other. There were no sudden moves. Both men continued to expose their hands for the other to see.

Two more steps and they were side by side, moving in opposite directions.

Fat mumbled, "S'happening brother."

Jimmy mumbled, "What's Sup, brother."

They cruised past each other into the night. Neither looked back.

JIMMY

His head, swollen like an overripe pumpkin, had been sewn and stitched from ear to ear. Lifeless, he resembled the cousin Harold remembered, except he was darker from the perpetual California sun. His huge swollen head was stitched from ear to ear, distorting his features.

Right away, Harold wished he hadn't seen his cousin. Would he ever be able to get the visual nightmare of Jimmy's head out of his head? He didn't think so.

He had not wanted to view the body!

"No!" he emphatically answered when asked.

The undertaker asked again.

Jimmy's sister Katie refused to view her brother's body and everyone agreed. "Not Katie." She was already near the edge, close to a train wreck of major proportions. Simple tasks like eating and getting dressed had, in the last four days, become major events. Knowing what she knew, who she knew, the amount of hidden money, she was afraid. One minute, looking over her shoulder for someone to shoot her, the next moment she would be crying hysterically.

Harold's mom, Clara, and her brother James, Jimmy's aunt and uncle, both said, "No thanks." They'd flown all the way from Alabama for the funeral. Viewing the violent death up close was a memory they did not want to take back home. Uncle James defended his actions with, "I remember the day he was born."

Jimmy's dad would have done the viewing but he was off being interviewed once again by the homicide detectives. The other

California cousins were making funeral arrangements.

It was left to Harold, the cousin from Alabama, to view the body and then to tell everyone how good his dead cousin looked. Except he didn't, "Damn Jimmy," he thought.

He'd gotten the call in Birmingham from his dad, Jimmy's uncle. Jimmy was dead at thirty-two. Gunned down in LA, on Sunset Boulevard in Hollywood. "What happened?" everyone questioned over long distance phone lines. "Why had it happened?" From Los Angeles, the answer came, "The cops were piecing it together."

Harold's last conversation with his cousin at 1:45 on a Friday morning, three months before, was haunting. Jimmy was high on something and not recognizing the two-hour time zone difference. He wanted and needed to talk. He searched for answers to the complex questions of his life.

Harold rose up in his bed and they talked.

Ten years apart, they had taken separate roads but they were blood, with Harold the elder always making himself available for his younger cousin. "We're double first cousins," they would brag. They were in fact. Harold's father and Jimmy's father were brothers. Their mothers were sisters. They were close.

Over the phone, Jimmy was troubled. He'd cry, flash anger, and talk of wanting to "start over."

"How are things down there?" he questioned. "I could open a business there. You think we could get some cheap real estate?" he wondered.

"Come on down, we'll get you clean and talk about what's next," encouraged Harold.

"I don't trust you," Jimmy responded.

. . . . .

The thugs drove up on Jimmy and caught him, literally, with his pants down, taking a shit.

He'd driven his new Mercedes, the metallic blue sport one with the wheels and the whole accessory package, in to see his man, old Walt, the mechanic. Walt was the best mechanic in the Valley. He had an old neighborhood garage where he also lived.

Walt was tinkering under the hood of Jimmy's car when the thugs arrived. The question of whether Walt was caught off guard, totally unaware, was afraid to speak up, or just didn't know anything, was never answered.

The thugs pretended they were glad to see Jimmy while ushering him out of the bathroom and into the back seat of their car. They held a pistol to his back. "Walt, we're giving Jimmy a ride. Be back later."

The questions were plentiful.

Shouldn't Walt have known? Couldn't he see the look of terror on Jimmy's face, the fear? Why did it take three big guys to escort one little guy? Why didn't Jimmy call out to Walt that they were thugs? Was he afraid they would shoot him right there? Did he think he might escape them later? Did he feel they would not harm him? Didn't Walt let Jimmy use the phone earlier to call a ride? Did Walt realize something was wrong when the ride showed up and Jimmy and the three thugs were long gone?

The thugs, high on rock cocaine, and without a plan, drove Jimmy all over Sylmar, Pacoima, and the north San Fernando Valley. "God damn it, we want the money," Ricardo, the dark skinned rail thin leader, demanded. They twice drove to Jimmy's apartment, the one he shared with his wife and daughter. They ransacked the place the first time, netting only a couple of thousand dollars. That pissed them off. They knew there was more.

"Where's the money?" Ricardo hissed.

The second time they went back to Jimmy's apartment, they whipped him into admitting there was more money. He gave up an additional five grand he had hidden in one of his cars.

. . . . .

Jimmy had paroled out of Chino the previous Sunday. Katie had been there to pick him up. They were always there for each other.

Their mom died when Katie was in tenth grade and Jimmy was in sixth. Their dad worked two jobs, to afford the house, the kids, food, and his Cadillac. He worked the 11pm to 7am graveyard shift on one job and then reported to his day job from 8 to 4. The rest of the time, he needed to sleep in order to continue the grueling routine.

The children learned to fend for themselves.

The younger brother took responsibility for the older sister. He screened her dates, and while his Dad slept between jobs, he hustled on the streets stealing for the older criminals.

By the time Jimmy finished high school, he was making more money than his Dad on both jobs and supporting his sister full time. College was out of the question for the both of them.

Since her mom died, Katie had been scared of everything; noises, open doors, and especially, darkness. Death had sneaked up on her Mom by way of a stroke, and Katie was afraid Death would at any time come looking for her. Jimmy, a player in the dope business, multiplied her fears. The dark, sharp knocks at night, cars next to her at the corner stoplight, a ring of the phone, anything could send chills through Katie. Jimmy became her security blanket. He made her feel safe and secure. She stayed out of his business, didn't ask questions, and he took care of everything.

.....

As boys, they had all grown up playing ball together, Jimmy, Ricardo, Lil' Red and Jonah. As young men, they'd earned their street credibility boosting cars, chopping them up and selling the parts, then having the "victim" file a claim with his or her insurance and they would divide up the money. As adult males, they'd spent time in prison together.

The thugs ransacked the apartment again, throwing things around just because they could. They ripped out the phone lines and took the new cell phone Jimmy had bought for his wife. They found the keys to Jimmy's other Mercedes, Lil' Red drove it away, and returned without it.

Jimmy sat on the couch, plotting how he could escape. Ricardo made small talk with Jimmy one minute and the next he'd hold the gun to his head and threaten his life.

Jimmy calculated his time, waiting for a moment, the right moment.

Jimmy knew Lil' Red and Jonah were scared of him. They were punks, jealous punks. Ricardo wanted more than Jimmy's money and cars. Ricardo wanted Jimmy's status. He wanted the respect Jimmy got in the neighborhood, the love Jimmy got from other thugs, and even from the cops. He knew he'd never get it with Jimmy around. "That yellow nigger think he better than us," Ricardo would say behind Jimmy's back.

The kidnapping had been Ricardo's idea of payback for a sour deal between the two where Ricardo felt Jimmy got the better of the deal. There were two sides to the story and the two sides never jived. Jimmy said things were squared away. Ricardo held on to the grudge.

Jimmy had been out of prison five days, when they drove up on him that Thursday morning, literally wiping his ass and forced him into the car.

There were other questions. "How did they know Jimmy was out? "Was Ricardo working with the cops?" It was common knowledge on the streets that one of the detectives, a Howard Lacey, was out to get Jimmy. Did he tip Ricardo that Jimmy was out? Would he turn his back on finding Jimmy's killer?

"Where's the money?" Ricardo demanded waving the 45-automatic in Jimmy's face.

"That's it," Jimmy responded. "I've been in prison," he continued sarcastically.

Ricardo lashed out with the weapon across Jimmy's face, opening a deep gash on his left cheek. Crimson blood gushed up and then out of the laceration.

"You fuck." Ricardo shot at Jimmy.

They drove Jimmy around to the two stash houses Jimmy owned and the other apartment he rented. The houses were used to cook the powder cocaine into rock. The apartment was the distribution center that Jimmy used to sell cocaine in Pacoima, Sylmar, and all across Los Angeles' San Fernando Valley.

The thugs found no more dope or money.

Jimmy's mind raced, "if, if, if…"

Ricardo, sensing Jimmy's thoughts, slapped him hard across the mouth for no apparent reason. "Yellow ass punk," he sneered.

. . . . .

Jimmy's fair skin came from his grandfather who was damn near white and grandmother, who often "passed" for white in segregated Alabama. She had been a mix of white and Native American. She'd married a light skinned black man thus making them, in American society, black. Like his grandfather, Jimmy was short, had a pug nose, and a mean streak that most men feared.

The cousins, Harold, Katie, and Jimmy, grew up like sisters and brothers until Katie and Jimmy's parents joined the great black migration in the 50s and 60s to the west and California.

Los Angeles moved at warp speed, while Birmingham inched along and often times moved backward. The cousins grew to be different. As adults, their visits became fewer and fewer, with Harold venturing out to California more so than the Californians returning home.

On Harold's last visit he'd spent more time with Katie than Jimmy. He'd witnessed Jimmy buying a kilo of coke and slapping the living piss out of one of his runners. Harold drew the familial line at the drugs and dangerous lifestyle.

. . . . .

They drove Jimmy into Hollywood and onto Sunset Boulevard. The thugs found an alleyway next to an almost empty parking lot. Overhead was a giant billboard advertising the latest hot television show. Jimmy noticed the billboard but did not know the show. They parked. Lil' Red and Jonah sat in the front seat. Ricardo sat in the back with Jimmy, the automatic weapon still at Jimmy's head. Ricardo whined on about the money but Jimmy swore "on my mother's grave" that was it.

"Two fucking cars and seven thousand dollars," Ricardo spit back at Jimmy.

They'd forgotten to search Jimmy's pockets. Ricardo did and found an additional five hundred dollars. "Bitch," Ricardo violently cracked the pistol across Jimmy's head. Jimmy whimpered, his hands covering his head. Blood trickled through his fingers and down his face. Ricardo opened the back door and whacked at Jimmy's swelling head again with the pistol. "Get your punk ass out of the car."

Jimmy fell onto the blacktop parking lot.

Jimmy rolled over, one of his teeth; covered with blood, fell from his mouth. He looked up at the sneering Ricardo. There was no doubt in his mind he was going to kill Ricardo. He had never killed anyone. He wouldn't go that far, a slap, a hit, maybe. But, there was no doubt, he was going to smoke Ricardo's ass. Ricardo would be his first.

. . . . .

"I don't trust you," Jimmy had repeated in the late night call to Harold. "I know you would take care of the money, but everything would have to be in your name and I don't know."

"Then put it in your dad's name." Harold urged.

Jimmy slurred his words. He was high on drugs and now sleepy. Silence intervened. Harold waited. He knew Jimmy was being vulnerable with the one person he could. At twenty-five hundred miles and another lifetime away from Jimmy's world, Harold was safe to talk to. Harold waited.

Jimmy's muted whimpers could be heard above the silence.

"Whitey Ford," Harold broke the silence. It was the name he had given Jimmy as a little league baseball pitcher. The name actually belonged to a former big league pitcher for the New York Yankees. Jimmy loved baseball and had been a helluva pitcher. Small with large hands, Jimmy would wrap his long fingers and big hands around a baseball, and he could make it dart, dip and slide in and around home plate. Everyone predicted he would be the family's athlete. But he took a detour with no U turns. His first fast buck on the streets meant the end of baseball.

"I know you're telling me right," Jimmy cried above the static in the phone.

.....

The alley to the parking lot was deserted. A little boy, dribbling a new basketball and wearing white Chuck Taylor Converse basketball shoes stood across the street. The boy saw Jimmy in the parking lot. The thugs did not see the boy.

Pop! Pop! Pop!

The scream raced loudly and involuntarily from Jimmy's mouth!

"AAAWWWWWWWWW!" he screamed.

The heat pierced his leg and stomach, burning his insides. Blood raced out of the hole in his pants and the tear in his shirt. Ricardo had shot him twice and missed once. The momentum of the shot hurled Jimmy backward across the parking lot. Jimmy fell, hitting his head on the pavement. CRACK! He tried to rise and momentarily passed out.

The thugs rolled off down the alleyway, never seeing the young boy watching all the time. They needed to get back to the safety of the valley right away.

Jimmy stirred. His leg moved, so did his upper torso. He was dazed and in shock but he rose up on shaky legs. Had he been coherent perhaps he would not have risen.

It was a mistake.

Ricardo looked back.

On wobbly legs Jimmy started toward the little boy. The little boy would help him. "Help," he tried to say but there wasn't enough strength for a word.

He stumbled.

The boy stood there. Watching, no longer dribbling.

Oblivious, tourists from around the world walked the nearby streets in their quest to see a movie star. They didn't see the drama unfolding a few feet away.

"Stop the car," Ricardo commanded. Lil' Red stopped the car. Ricardo jumped out. He ran to Jimmy. Jimmy struggled to stay on his feet. Ricardo ran up behind him. He placed the gun to Jimmy's head and pulled the trigger.

The little boy was the last thing Jimmy would see.

.....

The little boy would describe to the police the noise of the gun and the eruption of Jimmy's head in bloody pieces across the parking lot. Unafraid, the little boy also identified Ricardo, Lil' Red and Jonah and the make and model of the car.

.....

The subject had come up as easily as it had in the movie *The Godfather* about 1950's mobsters. Harold questioned, "Put a hit on them?"

He realized his California cousins were serious.

"We need five thousand dollars," Katie relayed. "I know who did it and I know who to get to take care of it."

. . . . .

The cemetery on the mountainside overlooking the valley was exquisite. The lush green lawn nestled into the mountain terrain. The day could not have been clearer or prettier.

At the gravesite, Jimmy's dad wept. He'd lost his only son. The Valley had changed. It was not the same place of opportunity he and his siblings had migrated to in the 1960s. He'd never second-guessed himself about leaving Birmingham, thirty years ago. Hell, he couldn't find a job. Still, in the 1990s he wondered. Would his wife and son still be alive? His wife had died from the stroke but would living in Birmingham have made a difference?

Harold was a pallbearer. His mind raced. Yes, he thought, Jimmy had broken laws but no one, least of all a thug, had the right to cold bloodily take his life. He pictured the swollen pumpkin of a head, stitched from ear to ear. The visual was stuck in his head and would be for a long time.

What would happen to Katie? Who would take care of her? What happened to the money? There should have been thousands? Did Katie know? Did Jimmy's dad? Did his wife?

Harold forced himself not to care. He figured he would not be coming back to Los Angeles for a while, maybe ever.

. . . . .

Surprising even himself, Harold came up with the cash for the hit. He put the questions out of his mind. He put the thought of what he had just done out of his mind. No one knew, but Katie. He would mail Katie a check from Alabama, labeling it marketing which was a reasonable expense in his business. He had Katie draw up a logo he would never use. He'd made sure there were no other connections to him. "No one had the right to kill my cousin," he reasoned. Harold bought a gun. He got a permit to carry it.

The sun rose high in the sky. The family looked down on Jimmy one last time. The minister ended with an "Amen," and the attendants with their white gloves and somber faces, lowered Jimmy's casket into the California hillside next to his mom.

Coach

Coach took it all in. Footballs spiraled upward, projectiles hurling toward the indoor roof. Wide receivers, like racehorses, pranced on fast feet. Offensive linemen grunted like hogs feeding at the trough. Defenders eager to crush someone worked themselves into a maddening froth.

The enemy dressed in yellow and gold, their shiny yellow jacket symbol plastered across their helmets, grunted, snorted, pranced, and pumped adrenaline in return.

Coach stood in the middle of the fifty-yard line, his feet firmly planted in the logo of the Alabama Tech Spiders. His black Spider's cap was pulled low over his eyes, which were covered by deep dark tinted shades. Coach sported his own Nike brand of shoe. The designer shirt tucked into his fitted coach's pants accented his well-built body. Cameras and flashbulbs clicked and flashed all around him.

Coach could have been a Hollywood star.

The new controversial domed stadium in downtown Birmingham, Alabama rocked with excitement. The pomp and circumstance of the televised game played out before national television cameras. The "Game Day" television crew primped for the make-up people. The sold out crowd of seventy two thousand color-coordinated fans; some drunk on alcohol, others drunk on the historic moment, worked themselves into a frenzy. Shirtless fraternity boys paraded colored signs declaring "STING THE YELLOW JACKETS," and "SMASH THE SPIDERS".

The Alabama Tech fans danced to James Brown's "Say It Loud—I'm Black and I'm Proud." "Say it loud," the Tech band bellowed above the music. "I'm Black and I'm Proud," came the response from the

Tech fans.

The Birmingham Post Dispatch morning headline of September 5, 2012 described it as, *The Day That Saves Birmingham*. The paper read *"…The debut of the new coach and the unveiling of the domed stadium in beleaguered downtown Birmingham will finally erase the 'Johannesburg of the South' reputation Birmingham deservedly earned in the 1960's during its days of civil rights demonstrations and church bombings.*

No one in the state of Alabama would forget this day.

"Hey Coach," the zebra striped black umpire with a huge grin on his face called out. The umpire gave Coach a fist bump.

"You ready for today?" he asked.

Coach grinned and nodded.

The two men faced off.

The umpire's eyes flashed hope and faith rewarded.

Coach's eyes said he understood.

A young female public relations representative hustled six cameramen onto the field. The cameramen snapped photos of the coach until the PR woman, checking her expensive Spiders watch, hustled the cameramen off the field.

Coach understood.

He had become a celebrity the day he was hired. Paul D. Jones, son of a mill worker, the first black Head Coach at Alabama Tech, the first black Head Coach at a major Southern University football factory in the state of Alabama, had become the sports story of the young twenty-first century. At Alabama Tech, Coach would have had a legitimate shot at the conference crown and the BCC national championship. At Tech, he'd be able to recruit the players needed to do both. No less was expected.

Alabama Tech's reputation as one of the longstanding powers of college football could make that happen.

. . . . .

The day he got the call compared with the day he married his wife Jayne and the day five years later, when his son, Jalen, was born. He felt lucky and blessed.

Coach had been an All American quarterback at Illinois. Over the last five years he'd led tiny Henderson College in Illinois to the Division II national championship three times. The two years they didn't win the championship they finished second.

Other schools called. Coach hired an agent. Most of the perennial losers knocked on his door. The bigger schools that courted him were the underdogs from the Pac 10 and Conference West. But Coach had learned patience from his dad, who'd worked thirty-five years in the mill on the same job. Just like during his playing days when, as a small high school southern boy from Louisiana, he'd held out for a school that would let him play quarterback, he held out for a school where he would have a chance to win it all and he knew he could win it all at Alabama Tech.

He'd had to convince his wife, Jayne Jones, biracial and middle class from Chicago, that they could move south. She had met her husband in college. She was a beautiful and brainy woman who would pursue a doctorate in education. He was the football star, the quarterback, and later the Coach. They became a dynamic duo.

A dean at Henderson College, Dr. Jayne, as she was known, had no desire to live anywhere near the state of Alabama. She had learned to tolerate Louisiana. When she traveled there with her white mother, she got stares of disbelief and the prolonged looks that ignorance breeds. She'd never been to Alabama and like most people, when it came to the state, she made her judgment on history and hearsay. She refused to consider it.

Coach turned the job down.

He underestimated the Alabama Tech President, Mark Warren. Warren, a liberal even in his college days at Tech, where as president of the student body, he, by himself, picketed the local country club when he found out his black friends were prohibited from playing golf there, would not give up. He insisted on heading up a one-man committee to hire the coach, that one man, being himself and he further insisted Paul was "the best fit for the job." Privately, he told Paul, "It's time and you're the guy to do it."

Warren walked a slippery slope and he knew it. If this move turned out to be a mistake his career was over. A calculating man, Warren was also at that point in his career where he was ready to go out with a big bang. He had his sights on his man and he was going to get him.

Warren called mornings, afternoons, and nights. The answer was always the same. No! Warren was tactical; he called the house line, increasing his chances of speaking with Jayne and Jalen. Unleasing his charm, in a voice as southern as grits and sweet as molasses, Warren assured them all that, "Coach Paul is our man."

He refused to interview anyone else.

Coach intrigued, did his homework. He made a list of pros and cons. There were many pros and one big con, the issue of race.

He talked to coaches, black and white. They typically responded.

"Why put yourself and your family through that?"

"This isn't just about race, this is about a college football culture that dominates the way of life. It's religion."

"You won't have a private moment."

"You will never be able to meet the expectations."

Coach consulted his dad. "Go for it if you want it," his dad encouraged. His mother-in-law told him "Follow your heart."

Now sure of his answer, Coach again told Warren "No."

Warren turned loose the big guns on his coach. He recruited the rich boosters who fueled the football program, the good ole boys. They announced they "didn't want to deal with no damn civil rights interviews and all that shit." The boosters also warned, "If he turns out to not be worth a shit, you can never fire him. Fire a black guy and it'll bring up all that civil rights shit again."

Warren refused to listen. He enjoyed great support from the student body, the faculty, and the board of trustees. They saw the benefits Coach could bring to the University. Warren had the whip hand.

Warren informed the boosters. Either it was Jones or he would hire a Yankee, someone totally unrelated to the program that would cut off the good old boys access to the athletic department. The boosters bowed.

The boosters threw money at Coach Paul like it was government cheese. They committed their considerable weight on any issue he might need help with. Coach could bring any assistant coaches he wanted, including the two black offensive and defensive coordinators who had been his long time friends. Privately, Coach raised the issue of black quarterbacks and the quarterback controversy that follows an average black quarterback versus an average white quarterback who earns his job and keeps it throughout his career. He reminded them that the school had not recruited him as a quarterback.

In a week's time, it was over.

The offer included a comparable job offer for Dr. Jayne, private schools for Jalen, promises of cars, and offers of housing. And Coach could run his program the way he wanted to.

It was an open-ended offer.

It would be a family decision.

Jalen made the call. "Dad, I want you to go there," he announced one evening. "Let's try it."

With Jalen on board, Dr. Jayne Ok'd the deal. The family braced for the impact. Paul called Mark Warren. "We're coming," he announced.

"Yesss," Warren shouted back into the phone!

Coach's agent said it was the easiest deal he'd ever done.

The support for coach was overwhelming. The Jones' received a telegram of congratulations from President and Mrs. Obama. Congratulatory DVDs arrived from elementary and high school aged students from all over the state of Alabama. Coach quickly became more powerful and popular than any Alabama politician or preacher. Dr. Jayne became more than a doting first lady, she would have a major say in the school's education department.

The media frenzy spun out of control. The scrutiny of Coach was worse than that of President Obama's first term. After all, to many this job was bigger than the presidency anyway. Everyone had to interview the Coach. His every word was nit-picked and interpreted. Coach was daily chatter for the Internet blogs; Like a Hollywood star, it mattered where Coach ate his meals, where he got his haircut. Old elementary school friends were dug up for interviews. No stones were left unturned.

Inevitably, as always with media darlings, it turned ugly.

Before he ever coached his first game at Tech, a former player from Henderson accused Coach of being a "pimp" who did not care about his players. "He's just in it for the money," the player alleged.

A couple of Henderson co-eds interviewed on Fox news created headlines with unsubstantiated and untrue rumors that Coach had fathered a child by a white undergraduate student at Henderson. The co-ed had been Jalen's baby sitter. In the ensuing conference media day session, a slimy talk show host asked Coach point blank if he could prove he did not father the girl's child. Coach and the University took the unprecedented step of arranging with the girl's parents to bring her to Birmingham, calling their own press conference and showing the girl was not pregnant. There were no adoption records. There was no child.

In national and international media, Coach's story crossed over beyond sports. Coach's story was featured in the *Wall Street Journal, Fortune,* and *People.* On the Internet Coach was "The Most Interesting Man in College Sports." Feature articles focused on how Alabama had run an end run around the rest of the country and hired an African American to hold a position that brought the status formerly held by icons like Bear Bryant, Shug Jordan, Nick Saban and Pat Dye. Internet chat rooms were off the chain.

Alabama media patted themselves on the back. The state was "moving forward" with a new domed stadium and the number one coach in the land "who just happened to be black."

Everyday, Coach hit the ground running, winning over the people with his honesty and straightforwardness. He visited over fifty booster clubs in the first two months on the job. He found that south of the city the clubs were all white, and in the city they were all black. He and Dr. Jayne found the same things with the schools and churches.

The white and black groups also wanted different things from him. The white groups were interested in winning, period. Winning games was the mandate. There would be no grace period. No replenishing the depleted recruiting stock. "Win, and win now was the mantra."

The black groups saw a historical milestone. The black group meetings were more like revivals, with gospel singing, and people praying over the new coach. Coach took home more fried chicken dinners than he could ever eat.

Early on, Coach proved he could recruit and not only the top black kids. He signed the top white kid out of the state of Alabama beating both Auburn and Alabama. The white kid, Raymond Baugh, said, "I want to be a part of it." His mom, an Auburn graduate, and his dad, an Alabama graduate, echoed the sentiment. His mom said on television, "We fell in love with Coach Paul."

Coach said the right things at booster club meetings. He said the right things on ESPN. He looked great in the gold and purple of Alabama Tech. His wife and son were adjusting and happy. Jayne had declared Birmingham's hills and greenery as "beautiful." She was also pregnant. Coach had the job of a lifetime.

Coach still would have to win many of the big money boosters over. There were still many private social functions where neither he, nor they, felt comfortable having him there. He was "not one of them." They were stuck in the "the good ole days" and in private it was whispered that Coach was not humble enough, not grateful enough. "Uppity."

Coach had to win. Nothing else mattered. And for them, he had better win every game.

. . . . .

Jimmy Jackson, a quarterback, the fastest player on the team, and barring injury a sure fire All American and future NFL player ran up to the Coach, his gold grill shining in his mouth. Jimmy had been Coach's first big signee. Coach had won over his grandfather, Truck, and had stolen him from both Auburn and the University of Alabama. The two traditional schools were unsure about Jimmy's background and hesitated when Jimmy, who in their minds fit wide receiver better than quarterback told them he wanted to start at quarterback for three years, and would not play wide receiver. Coach saw his own potential in Jimmy. He assured Jimmy and Truck that Jimmy was a quarterback.

"Good luck Coach," Jimmy grinned. Coach offered a fist bump. Jimmy wrapped him up in a bear hug. "We're gonna get them for you Coach," he whispered in Coach's ear.

. . . . .

Coach Paul wanted the game to start. *Hurry!* he thought, staring at the clock.

The last few minutes had been a blur. The teams left the field for their last meeting with the coaches. Coach walked off the field with Jalen, the surreal scene reeling through his mind. He safely tucked the images away for a Saturday, decades from now, when he would look back.

He decided to low key it with the boys. They were ready. He didn't want to overhype the situation. The players sat attentive, nervous, twitching, every eye on their Coach.

Coach finished with, "We're all in it together. When we look back, we'll appreciate what we do today, together."

Running onto the field Coach Paul was stopped for the customary ESPN interview. It was anything but customary. The long-winded sideline reporter, a blond woman too hyped up in the moment, wound around and around before coming to the question she had been prepped to ask, "How does it feel today to be opening a new domed stadium and to be a head football coach at Alabama Tech in the state of Alabama?" Coach Paul gave the right answer. "It will feel better when we win."

Coach wanted to win. He needed to win. All the pomp, circumstance, good will, and money would mean nothing if he didn't win. Coached had ditched his phone early that morning as it continually rang, buzzed, and vibrated with call, e-mail and texts. His mentor from his college days, the legendary Bobby Windom, the winningest coach in college football, reminded him to "Focus on the game. Nothing else matters."

Coach eyed the clock. He wanted it to move. He needed it to move. "Let's get the game started," he thought. He found Jayne in the stands on the fifty-yard line. She had turned down the chance to sit in the boxes with the dignitaries. Jayne reminded them, "We didn't have boxes at Henderson." Mark Warren and his wife, Betty, sat next to Jayne. Mark was as happy as the day he'd finally integrated the country club.

Coach didn't see Jalen. Where was Jalen?

Jalen found his dad. Running up to Coach he hugged his dad and would not let go. Jalen's new best friend Toby, Mark Warren's grandson, joined in what became a three-way hug.

"Ready Daddy?" Jalen asked. Coach held on tightly to his son, and Toby. The ESPN cameras captured the moment. A tear mustered its way into Coach's eye. Coach pushed his son and Toby back before the tear could fall. He could not tear up here in front of thirty million people on prime time television.

The thud of the kickoff sent the leather spiral of a ball sailing end over end in the lights of the dome. Coach, relieved, watched the ball twirl. Finally, the game had started.

About the Author

Thom Gossom, Jr. is a writer, actor, and film producer. His memoir, *WalkOn: My Reluctant Journey to Integration at Auburn University*, is his story as the first African-American athlete to graduate from Auburn. Additional works include a critically acclaimed play, *Speak Of Me as I Am*, and his blog, *As I SEE It*.

The Slice of Life Collection of short stories continues with *Another Slice of Life* and *The Rest of The Pie*.

On television, Gossom starred as Israel, the title character in the Emmy® winning *NYPD Blue* episode, "Lost Israel." Other credits include *Containment, Fight Club*, and *Jeepers Creepers 2*.

Gossom produced the public television documentary film *Quiet Courage.*

To inquire about a possible appearance please contact him at

www.BestGurl.com or facebook.com/BestGurlinc

CPSIA information can be obtained at www.ICGtesting.com
Printed in the USA
LVOW08s0420090816

499540LV00001B/5/P

9 780997 199659